Reflex and Bone Structure

Books by Clarence Major

Reflex and Bone Structure
The Syncopated Cakewalk
The Dark and Feeling
NO
The Cotton Club
Symptoms and Madness
Private Line
Dictionary of Afro-American Slang
Swallow the Lake
The New Black Poetry
All-Night Visitors

Reflex and Bone Structure

by

Clarence Major

Fiction Collective   New York

First Edition
Copyright © 1975 by Clarence Major
All rights reserved
Library of Congress Catalog number: 75-10746
ISBN: 0-914590-17-0 (paperback)
ISBN: 0-914590-16-2 (hardcover)

Typesetting by   New Hampshire Composition
Concord, New Hampshire

Published by   FICTION COLLECTIVE

Distributed by   George Braziller, Inc.
One Park Avenue
New York, New York 10016

This publication is in part made possible with support from
the New York State Council on the Arts, and with the
cooperation of Teachers and Writers Collaborative and
Brooklyn College.

Thanks to Sharyn

This book is an extension of, not a duplication of reality.
The characters and events are happening for the first time.

Reflex and Bone Structure

1
A Bad Connection

Cora is putting on a dress. It's blue with white flowers. Her lips are pressed tightly together.

Canada is leaning with his back against the mirror and Dale is leaving. I *think* he's leaving. He's headed for the door.

We're all at a party suddenly. Place full of cranks dumbbells failures showoffs playgirls juveniles boozers fallen-angels chatterboxes twotime losers meanies snobs, you name it. Canada is drinking a lot and Cora is beginning to flirt. She's in a musty hallway with someone. Dale is in the toilet letting his horse out to pasture. Cora wants to go play pony express with somebody. I smile, they smile.

The scattered pieces of the bodies were found.

I bake a Middle Eastern dish of eggplant, cheese and rice. Cora and I eat it.

Later, we make love on the table with the dishes beneath us, sliding around, falling and breaking. We're happy.

Naked together on the floor, we pinch each other and giggle for hours.

I saw some of the work the cops did. One used a flat device to take the fingerprints. Since rigor mortis hadn't set in the spoonlike object wasn't necessary. I helped them. Canada helped too. Everybody in the neighborhood pitched in and gave a hand. They all got their fingerprints taken. Though no one had counted on that. The cops had fingerprint cards they carried in a plastic briefcase along with one of those syringes for injecting silicone beneath the skin. This way prints can be taken effectively. The cops were all over the place looking in crevices. They looked beneath the bed and in the empty closets. They had some desensitizing fluid they didn't use.

These policemen were real. They were very funny. Canada was once a cop but I don't think he was ever as funny as these. One had a Polaroid MP-3 camera for copy work—the kind that gives an instant negative. He also carried in his pocket a bottle of ultraviolet ink. Another one wore rubber gloves and picked his teeth with a toothpick. Still a third moved around the place with a scalpel scraping up the blood. Dry spots. One was working on the edge of the window with a hacksaw. Why, I don't know. Another held test tubes for the one scraping up blood spots. One was sprinkling powder around the devastated area of the suitcase—rather, what was left of the suitcase. They'd already marked off what was left of the area with a piece of chalk.

But I didn't hang around.

Canada tries too hard sometimes. He tries to crack into Cora. Burst into Cora. Open Cora with his sledge-hammer. But I weave *around* the stern cathedrals in her holy city, her very pure spirit.

A man with wet purple lips tries to kiss Cora while my back is turned. Canada feels the man moving against the inner surface of himself. And Cora moves closer. Away.

She says he was just another victim out of the tropic rivers of his own brain. Strong but no skill. Plowing inside the image of his own maypole.

Cora's damp lips brush mine as she leaves.

The moment the door is closed I fall into a deep sleep.

And Cora listens to the foggy song of Canada's breathing. Her black eyelids blinking in darkness.

Immediately we're at another party. The lights are pink. All the people are well-dressed and drunk. Healthy cows and chickens are standing around in the living room, mooing and clucking. The people do not seem to be aware of them and they're not aware of the people. I'm the single exception. Even Cora, Dale and Canada can't see the animals. A red hen flies to the back of a fat, red and white cow. The chicken says, "Cluck, cluck cluck, cluck, cluck cluck, cluck cluck."

It's too much. I take Cora home in a taxi.

We're in bed watching the late movie. It's 1938. *A Slight Case of Murder.* Edward G. Robinson and Jane Bryan.

I go in the bathroom to pee. Finished, I look at my aging face. Little Caesar. I wink at him in the mirror. He winks back.

I'm back in bed. The late late show comes on. It's 1923. *The Bright Shawl.* Dorothy Gish, Mary Astor. I'm taking Mary Astor home in a yellow taxi. Dorothy Gish is jealous.

All afternoon I am still *seeing*. I see from the growing darkness of a room, out. There is an undulating human motion. Sawing and slushing back and forth. A radio is on and music is heard. This memory lodges in me like an Arabic mosaic.

I check the *TV Guide* for the early evening movie. I cannot get comfortable against a stack of pillows.

I'm lying against limbs and twigs. Still heavy-lidded with a hangover. Puckered lips touch my arm.

A relatively successful hack moves across the screen. An egomaniac. A wreck who is a dissenter yells at her. In another life she lives in a dingy apartment in the East 20s.

We wait through the unending mechanics and veneer of TV scheduled movies.

"There's a gentleman at the door to see you, Mrs. Webb."

Cora opens her thighs to let in the voice from the screen. I open my lazy thighs too. Cora lets the long talking tongue play between her legs. They are not twigs.

In long strokes she licks the swollen tight flesh. She passes out beneath wet delicious waves.

Yet something is very raw and empty behind the flurry of her spirit. The cool vacancy of her eyes.

Now. I begin to follow the plot. It is a thriller, yet it fails to thrill. I am involved with a frigid rich mother of a fucker. Who quickly inherits not simply material wealth after murdering Mrs. Webb but also the higher psychic understanding of power.

Canada picks up the phone. "This is a recording: The world is full of people who don't give a fuck about you. They would step over your broken body and stroll through your blood. The world is very full of people who do not give a shit about you. They would step through your blood any time. This is still a recording: The whole world is full of people who do not care one way or another about you. They would think nothing of your death. The world is full of people who do not care. The world is full of people who care nothing for you. The world is full of people who don't give a shit for you. The world is full . . .''

Cora turns on the television set. There is a program just starting called "The Inlet Game." In it, people have to guess what's going to happen next. All the action takes place in the doorway of the television studio.

Cora switches to a children's program. It's all about P and Y and B and T and G and F and H and E and W and C. It's all about the deep dark secrets of the mind. A boy and a girl are exploring a haunted castle called Alphabetical Africa. They stop in a sideroom to watch reruns of their own lives. A monster down the hallway is laughing. This they can hear clearly. They shake with fear, holding each other for comfort. At this point a toy commercial comes on.

Cora has become a big time movie star! I'm in the dentist's waiting room. A variety of magazines are on a table. A picture of Cora's face is on the cover of each one. The caption says: *The Brightest New Star in Ages! See page 10!* I open one to page ten and there's a full-page book ad. Title of book: *Reflex and Bone Structure.*

As a child she was a nymphet and she still is attracted to children. Boys.

One boy in a washed out green cotton shirt. He looked ironed and crammed into it. Dark hands and pockets with holes in them. He hung around the stairway. Under muddy yellow lights.

Cora says, "He looks at me with hunger."

Such stubborn begging eyes. Sometimes she shakes a playful finger at his nose. He blushes. His dimples reach the smooth projection of his chin. He lives downstairs behind the blue door on the right, and even number.

He follows her up the stairway. He plays as he climbs. He peeps under her skirt. She peeps under her own skirt. Canada runs his hand under it.

I run my eyes over her. I begin to play with a notion. The hallway as always smells of fresh piss. People stop here out of desperation in crucial moments.

The boy's mother is as big as a washtub. She rushes up to Cora with a butcher knife. She starts slicing tomatoes, taking them, one at a time, from her apron pocket.

I stab my fear and stash it under the flower pots. Meanwhile I feel an inner shivering. I want to fornicate with a precious woman. Cora's eyes are troubled.

She winks one eye at the boy and he assumes correctly that he is to *have* and be *had*. To enter Sodom and Gomorrah. To retrace his way to worshipped nipples.

Everything and nothing rapidly occurs to Cora. If Canada is already home she will simply invite the young neighbor to have hot chocolate or supper or both.

But I am already here.

Canada comes in listening to his own footsteps. Leaving tracks. He puts down a brown paper bag. Yet he couldn't remember what it contained. But since it was moving, it obviously held something live. A puppy a bird what.

The boy nervously licks the corky dark ridges of his own lips. The door to the kitchen opens. Cora takes the live thing in the bag back into the kitchen.

The thing leaves the bag and crawls up Cora's naked thigh and lodges itself snugly near her cunt. In the hair. Like a tick.

Canada is laughing with the child. But I cannot laugh. I have work to do. It is my salvation. And I keep them all moving going coming around, even when they don't care.

Cora changes clothes. She has taken a shower and now wears her white nylon gown with matching white panties. She is all soft texture and quivering flesh.

The boy licks Canada's earlobe then feels embarrassed. Somebody in the hallway is running down the stairway. The walls vibrate. The soft splash of cars going by in the rain on the street below. The window is closed. It should be open. Particularly since Cora thought she opened it.

"Do you know what the fuck you're doing?"

"Yes, Canada."

Cora sprawls in the big arm chair from the Original Flea Market. She holds up two fingers in a V.

The boy grins. Broken teeth.

Cora throws a thigh over the arm of the antique chair and sighs. Her mind is shattered.

Blushing, I go over and, holding her by the shoulders, I carefully ply my tongue to the roots of her hair along the edges of her hairline. Her skull bone is very hard under the pressure. I stop as quickly as I start.

I move back across the room. The child has a dirty unwashed pissy odor. He moves in a circle around Canada while watching Cora. Canada, meanwhile, squeezes his own arms and his toes begin to wiggle in his sandals.

Cora says, "What I am trying to do is overthrow the desperation of each second. And to graft meaning that is never there onto them: with the living tissue of my being."

She thinks she's being profound as well as sexy.

The kitchen door is open.

She hasn't pulled down the shades in the kitchen, so the late afternoon sunlight splashes in on the rubber plants, all the way into the front where we are.

Across the street, at the window in another building sits stately an old man with the raw ability to endure his shitty shambles reading the *Daily News*. He now watches us. If he can see.

The sun shines and it is raining, so the devil beats his wife in hell. It is a symphony of murder. Harp honking and triumphant blare. French horns and pulsing dead monks. But what with this little hispanic moron angel who has followed Cora. Is it her mother impulse that attracts his salty nose.

He sticks his finger in his nose. He moves it like a piece of metal in a crucible. He turns away.

He stands before the mirror and blows up his cheeks. Watching our reflections.

Cora's flimsy garment floats and she catches its ends and, giggling, tucks them beneath her fists.

She winks an eye at the boy, and he winks back from the mirror.

Someone in the hallway shouts, "I'm going to trip in a pharmachological aircraft!" And obviously they are running upstairs double-time.

The boy opens his mouth and examines his teeth. Cora is scratching her kneecaps.

I am in control of myself and the situation.

Canada pretends he is asleep.

Cora says, "I am the president of the United Stiffs Atomic Cuntological Mission. A non-profit making organization." And she laughs.

The echo is inside me.

And the boy plays with the mirror. He's a baby goat.

Meanwhile I go into the kitchen and unload the pistol in the silverware drawer. Canada comes in.

In the shadows he looks bizarre. He reloads the gun and spins it. Checks it. One eye squinted. He's an expert.

"What'd you say?"

"I didn't say anything." Canada smiles.

"Oh. Guess I'm hearing things."

He pointed the gun at me.

"If you kill me a lot of people will start dying."

Canada laughs. "It's an electric screw driver. I simply want to fix the leak in the shower nozzle."

And in the other room we hear Cora laughing and, for some reason, the boy has started crying. Painful sobbing.

Here I go into the gun manufacturing business. I have the boy working for me. Cora is the business manager. Just the thing for her. Dale runs the warehouse. Canada is the salesman, travels everywheres. When sales are down we all cry together. When the business is up we party. Throw big parties. Dance and get drunk. Stay up all night. We're secure. We're even advertised in *Field & Stream*.

Late at night, I drive one of my own delivery trucks. I deliver thousands of pistols to Cora's apartment. Hide them all in the kitchen drawer.

I'm trying to pay attention to everything all at once.

As the author of this, I get the chance to visit the medical examiner's office and to go through his records. He is not a character but an idea. His office is an abstraction. Information on Cora and Dale is scribbled on sheets of paper, silently standing in files. It's a threat to the mystery.

Canada is a mystery behind his dark glasses. Clad in yellow ochre shirt and ivory black slacks. Standing beside the bed. As I move in a circle around the bed.

Cora's on the bed watching TV. She loves *I Love Lucy*. And if anybody involved in that skit wanted to look directly into her, they very well could.

"Can't you turn on?" Canada says.

Cora answers, "I did. And he got high. *Him.*"

Canada looks at me.

"Him?"

"Yes. Him."

"He got high when I turned on."

Canada gives me an unbelieving look. I still don't trust him. He's bad. I can handle Cora. She's elusive. Canada never changes so I know what to expect, and I don't like what I expect. Not from him.

I stop moving and Canada starts.

"You're going to split your pants."

"She's marvelous."

"Who?"

"Lucy."

"So am I," says Canada.

"Of course."

His naked right knee fell into the blue quilt. His face was menacing her.

"I'm going to eat you." He was growling.

Cora screamed. With laughter.

And Canada fell on the floor. He was getting a pot belly from too much drinking. He too was consumed by laughter.

"Everytime I see you, baby, you look better?"

"Who me."

"Who?"

Confusion confuses me and I refuse to answer. Fuck them both in their earlobes. I get sick of them. Bonnie-and-Clyde motherfuckers.

They give up on me. They should.

Before he throws her down, Cora feels the wet stab of Canada's tongue dig into her ear. She closes her eyelids. Wet slits. Each. And the great mounds of her rear end move.

Yet she has problems. It's the memory of her dead father and her dying mother. She never talks about them. I take that back. She talks about them too much.

I talk about too many things too much too. Sometimes I am sure I give too much space to Cora. Fuck Cora.

Canada fucks Cora.
Cora fucks Canada.

On second thought maybe I never noticed a thing. Cora asked me something and I said, "Oh, yes, I feel it." But what kind of answer is that. Especially when I don't know what she wanted to know.

She doesn't know either. Sometimes if she's half asleep she calls me Dale. I have almost no sense of Dale except I know I don't like him. He's good, too good. He's too far away to be bad.

Just how many secret trips Dale's stinky fingers made up or down Cora's lovely spine, perhaps, is not even *the* question. If there is a question. I break out on hot days in a cold sweat. Still, I find Dale absolutely filthy. You know how it is when you detest someone, and cannot make *how* you feel felt because there is no clear object to focus on, and no one who can understand exactly what causes your hatred. I used to imagine Dale was a fly and I, a cartoon character with a swatter sneaking up behind him, ready to get him and his stinking flyspeck. Too often, I'm tortured by a sense of dread caused by the fear that I do not really hate Dale, but respond this way to him out of a lack of interest. I mean, I *should* be interested in him since he's one of my creations. He *should* have a character, a personality. And it is strange that I'm jealous of him since he's formless. I lie when I say he won't let me explain him. He doesn't give a fuck about me: whether or not I give him presence or talk about him. He isn't shy. He simply doesn't know me.

I sent Dale out to North Dakota. I needed a break from him. He was caught in a duststorm. He ran in the wrong direction and a hoodoo fell on him. When a large column of earth like this falls on you, you can usually forget it. But Dale survived.

Right now he's looking for a part to play.

I'll tell you a little story about Dale. Based on all the people I've ever detested, he falls, face first, over into a cave. One without a bottom. I see myself walking firmly through his lack of substance. But if he is tangible, then what. Dale tried to sell house plants one year. He gave up acting. He threw himself on the mercy of the world, crawled around begging people to believe in him. You know what happened. He got shot in the ass with a bee bee gun. He found himself up shit's creek without a paddle.

"I'm not *going* to your place anymore, Cora. It has to be here or not at all. I don't like your landlady anyway. She looks down her nose at me. The old witch! If I go there again I might spit in her face—which might cause a sensation too expensive for my senses."

She sniffed at the urgency in my voice. Shut up nigger and fuck me."

I'd never called *her* by that affectionate name.

Canada came in. Said nothing. Bit his lip.

I cleared my throat.

She got up and kissed Canada.

"You're a good proselytizer, Cora"

"Thank you, Canada."

She had *that* look again. Sometimes she thinks her father can hear her see her touch and even love her. Something happens to her eyes at such moments. A delicate membraney mucous surface. A facial cove. Well. It serves her right.

There is reason to believe Canada is actively involved with the revolutionary group that staged the boobytrap. Obviously it was staged. But there is equal reason to believe Canada knew nothing of this particular mission.

Yet Canada has never indicated involvement with any revolutionary group. When would he have the time. But that is not what we mean. I see him as one who lives by his wits. And yet, I don't know how he lives. He is a renegade.

He probably has clandestine affairs too.

Cora, naked, does a few ballet steps before her mirror. She does not think her appearance beautiful, but from several angles it is. Depending on who looks. For example. I am looking on at the moment. We hear a key turning in the front door.

Someone hides in her closet. He fitted well behind the garments. His white eyes refusing to glow in the dark.

"Hello Dale."

And the high tide of Cora's laughter fills her apartment. The person in the closet is barefoot. Beneath his feet and between his toes is a slimy white substance that has left tracks, indicating his recent retreat.

But Dale, high, does not notice.

"Baby," Dale says, "before you take off your things would you go get some black walnut ice cream."

But she continues to dance. Aloof.

He threw up his hands. A helpless penguin trying to take flight. Dale stood, then began to move about the room. Soon he was walking in a loose circular motion.

Cora dances on her toes, watching herself carefully.

Dale goes and turns the lock. He's nervous.

I run the ice cream store. Tons of it are in the hallway. Dale has been bodily consumed by it. He's swimming upside down in a river of ice cream.

What else can I tell you? The future is not bright!

A rubber plant may be the guilty one. It seems silent

and moves only slightly. In its presence I talk to myself. My words are empty. My mind has gone into the plant.

Canada and Cora are visiting the Grand Canyon of the Colorado River. Arizona is good for them. A Mexican, Mr. Zodiac, is their guide. He tries to amuse them with things like, "Can you correlate while you congregate and copulate? Do you constipate or conjugate?"

Canada is driving a rented purple Ford. Cora's beside him. They're on the Cross County Expressway. A cop stops them. Canada shows the cop his American Express card. Says, "Charge it."

The cop takes the card, chews it into tiny peices then spits it into Canada's face.

"For that you will suffer." Canada is firm.

The cop falls on his knees and starts crying.

The boy has gone away but Canada wears his cheap green shirt. I don't get the point. Scarcely able to speak Canada is guilty of something.

His twisted face represses something. Perhaps desperation. His large and sad dark eyes offer me his unspoken sorrow. If he is acting it is artwork of a high order. If he speaks he will sound like himself.

I trust I am still intact. After he leaves I turn over in my mind. Yet I am not really qualified to think about anything or anybody. I have only what I can steal. And I have not stolen anything.

Or what comes to me accidentally. I can't explain

how anything relates to anything else. Or how a world war can erupt from conflict over a person as sex object.

I can't explain why I can't remember. Nor the presence of the word "freedom" in my vocabulary. Obviously I am purely and absolutely religious.

Cora is so exciting, yet, you can't do anything with her. She's like a tree. You can look at her. You can make her do nothing that does not comply with herself.

A tree. With green leaves you can chew.

Cora. She has sap.

A tree. You can rub your saliva into its gray wood. Watch it turn purple. Then blue. And possibly even pink. Wood is often as pink as pussy. Still it remains essentially untouched. It is only when you begin to approach it technologically, as an object, a thing of utilitarian possibilities, that it falls to pieces.

I haven't changed one degree in any direction.

And Cora waits for further instructions.

I am in a foreign country, in a tiny fishing village. A procession of natives, dressed in black, are following four pallbearers, also in black, carrying a coffin. They are moaning, climbing a hill, and the orange sun is going down behind them. I must have seen this somewhere. Cora is in the coffin. I step closer to make sure it's Cora. It is. She sits up, suddenly. The pallbearers drop their palls and run. The whole procession scatters.

The playbill in hand. It is damp from perspiration.

Cora learns her lines well. Good evening, folks. We are in the Concept West Village Theatre on Grove Street near Sheridan Square. In a few moments you will hear Dale's best strongest voice open the performance.

I am backstage. From where I am standing I see the shabby glow of a red outline. It is Dale's body. Cora isn't in sight but she knows her part. And she certainly isn't far away. I feel focused as rigidly as one crazed in a trance.

Cora suddenly appears. She is wearing a Fouke-dyed black fur seal coat with side buttons and great deep pockets! Beneath, there is nothing else. Every step she takes exposes her cunt. But she doesn't seem to care.

I simply refuse to go into details. Fragments can be all we have. To make the whole. An archaeologist might, of course, look for different clues. Somebody now taps me on the shoulder. The person is a nervous man I have never seen before.

"Don't worry. It will go fine."

"Yeah."

He scratches his keen black nose. He suddenly jerks his arm to see the face of his watch. It gives me a funny feeling.

Cora seems worked up to a throbbing conceit.

"And if she is a joke, shit, boy, I want to laugh, but good."

I remain in myself. The space around me: who does it belong to. The man who touched me still stands beside me. My breathing takes up a lot of room. I watch Cora's breasts.

They rise, they fall. Her conceit may be a cover for her insecurity. She needs to touch somebody, to be held. I need attachment. She is beautiful, I am magnificent. But now the curtains kick and begin sliding back.

The fundamental moment is upon us.

Something in me screams from neglect.

"It's a challenging play. Filthy as hell but it certainly should punch them right in the guts."

"Yes, you should be out front."

"My presence here."

"You understand."

"I saw the dress rehearsals."

"Keep me company."

"I'd like to do more than . . . "

"Would you like to do."

Many already were out front.

The crisp edge dropped from Cora's accent. Becoming sensuous. It causes me to shrivel. I look good in my tweed sport jacket and my creaseless colorless slacks but I am not happy. I am shriveling away.

Canada is somewhere in the back of my mind. He smells better than I smell. I have a mildew odor and I am growing old. Cora pretends not to notice my gray hair.

She likes unusual conditions.

What would I like.

Cora lets the wet tip of her tongue touch the dry area just inside my right ear. Between words.

"I go crunch crunch all over you."

"Right this minute?"

She smiles. Her hand is on my shoulder.

I watch the action on stage. No one is speaking. There are very few speaking parts. It is part of the drama's charm.

"You must have consideration."

The pressure of her mouth on mine cut off my flow of thoughts. My few words. She turns fully into my open arms.

"I feel," Cora says, "like a mean slut! I want to bite you. Obey you! Destroy you!"

I am me. And she knows it.

"I promise directly after the show."

"Don't promise anymore."

Meanwhile she opens her coat watching my eyes. With my middle finger I tickle her clit and she wiggles her ass. Grinning and clicking her tongue against her teeth. Cora does not realize she can be silly.

She is usually clandestine. I am usually me. My name is mine. Cora's secrecy is her own. Her deception is often an invention. It depends on how good I am.

"Not here. Back there."

"You remember the fairies in the tale."

"Which fairies in whose tail."

She remembers screaming. She follows the soft movements of his shadow. Dale had tried to insert his rancid big toe into her mouth. Half asleep. "Suck." The knobby extension wiggling her upper lip.

Even in here we hear the whispers as well as the shouts from the stage. Cora falls back, her backside on the edge of the dressing table. With the hard pressure of her tongue, she licks her lips. She scratches her thigh.

Above us is a naked light bulb I don't like. On the wall is a photo of a famous and cadaverous singer who is in the blues business. She looks like a man.

Cora has a high ass and big shapely legs. She's wearing her jacquard tapestry textured white print dress now. Having just changed. Carefree elegance. Chocolate ice cream.

My elbows on the dressing table begin to ache.

And someone opens the door. It's Dale who stands there, mouth open, watching us. I erase him. He's still on stage. In his glory. Cutting another notch into the totem pole of his career.

Dale opens the door again and this time he enters. His eyes buck and they shift and he looks around nervously. Cora gives him a bitchy look and murmurs something I am sure he does not hear. The imprints of his knees have made his pants look bowlegged.

"Ready."

And his eyes skip. His vision glides across my face then he lets it rest somewhere on the window glass. Between the interior and the night.

Dale goes to a police station, tells them he wants his fingerprints taken. They take him into a small sideroom and lock the door. "Strip," a cop says. Dale undresses and a dozen policemen lift him, holding him prone against the ceiling, rolling him along its surface. They keep this up for twenty-four hours. When they let him rest on the floor, he has turned into Cora.

Dale thinks he might be able to write a novel. The idea excites his imagination. He plans to call it, "The Complete History of Cora Hull's Vagina." Dale shakes the ice in his glass. He looks at Canada, who is on the opposite side.

"Vagina is not the word. Pussy or cunt."

The waitress overhears the conversation and coughs violently. She takes off her apron and runs to the kitchen.

Cora is toying with the idea of making a movie. Canada will star, Dale will co-star. Her working title is, "Cocky Motherfuckers of the Purple Saga Get Out of Town Before Sundown."

While Canada isn't looking Cora takes off for trips to areas of salt marsh and salt lakes. She runs her fingers through thick grass, and licks dew from leaves. She plays with hot springs and hoar frost. She irrigates lakes for poor farmers. She listens to her echo at the Devil's Tower in Wyoming. Cora collects wormwood. She explores the plumbing system of the world. She melts icebergs and swims in dust-wells. While watching the Midnight Sun, from the Arctic Circle, she ties a cyclone into a bowknot.

Cora's on the beach. Volcanic ash in her hair. She's turned deep black from tropical sunlight. She smells of peaches.

The play *Hades* ran into a second month. This was unusual because it was extremely bad. Very poor in quality. Particularly acting.

Everybody was jammed there. In high spirits.

I sat on the window ledge. Hogging the tiny breeze from the open window. Fire escape beyond the glass.

Some man dropped the dangling length of his arm around Cora. I closed my eyes. The pressure was building.

People are served Ritz crackers. And Wispride cheese. Blue and gold and greenish pink hegods and shegods. With black wine glasses.

Cora caught the twinkle in some strange man's eye. I traced a line on the ledge and turned fully to the night. Looking over the East River toward Brooklyn.

Outside the window I saw the man's childish grin. What was it about him that attracted Cora. The psychedelic lights continued to dance against moving faces.

From the turntable, *The Jimi Hendrix Experience* jumps through the room with the force of Goya dancers.

Cora prowls her way to the toilet and locks the door against intrusion.

She sees her private expression from the door mirror. While there is a light tapping on the other side.

"Yes, who's there."

"Are you really seeing Dale."

"You doubt it."

"Not that I doubt."

"Listen," Cora says, "no more."

And, as I continue to lean, my back against a downstairs wall, she takes vertical flight.

The wall is cold. I am stuffed with cocky heat. Cora now wears an orange leather minidress. As she flies.

Her fingers play with the soft hair of her own neck. The way I would do it. Someone upstairs is dancing. The music. The floor throbs.

"Talk."
"Talk to me."
"There's a better way to communicate, baby."

Dale kisses Cora's neck. He strokes her thighs. His fingers soon dance against the soft skin of her upper stomach between her ribs.

"Communication."
"Consciousness is the key."
They kiss again and again.

I am in someone's apartment. It is small, very narrow. It consists of two rooms with not much indication of a partition. The walls are rough white plaster. It is a terrible place to have to live. Yet whoever lives here must have to. Near the front window, with Dale mashed against her belly, her back flat against the wall, Cora receives his lovemaking with closed eyes. Her fingers are digging into his shoulders.

Dale's whisky-smelling breath swam into her. He was laughing and the ripple of his laughter shook Cora. His bony hand touched her exposed hip. He put pressure on her and the pressure spread.

And it continues to build and spread.

He let two of his fingers pry at her seams.

"What's this?"

His face was very close and Cora couldn't speak. I was watching because I couldn't do anything else. There was nothing better.

"What's what?"

"Say it often enough and see what happens to the idea."

"I command you."

"Pussy pussy pussy pussy pussy pussy pussy pussy pussy pussy pussy pussy pussy."

"That's enough."

Meanwhile he'd taken a long aim. But the shot was bad and he scratched his head.

"Another great accomplishment."

"It's nothing. You shouldn't chalk this one up in your score book."

"I never am that brutal."

"Then you tend to forget bad luck."

Dale beat his fist into his open palm.

"I may take up the guitar," he said.

His breathing continues to sound heavy.

Through the floor or from the hallway I can hear singer Wilson Pickett's recorded voice screaming from a turntable.

"I keep expecting Canada," Cora said.

"*Can* Canada!"

"Shit!"

Everything spoken seems to complicate my role. I am willing to change it. It frightens me often. The thought that I remain so suspicious. That I can't trust anyone. I *want* to trust. Or I will leave without collecting my broken pieces.

Canada comes in close suddenly and immediately pulls back. And starts to go away again.

"Come over here and get on your knees."

He doesn't move.

"I'm not a thing."

I settle in a nearby chair to watch and to listen. Canada licks an open sore on his arm. It instantly heals.

"Well. Come stand close."

"If you say I'm a winner."

"I say. I say it."

Cora is driving a stolen car. She is somewhere in Southeastern Connecticut, speeding, at three in the morning. Fog is thick. Her headlights are dim. She starts laughing and crying at the same time. The car crashes into the rear end of a truck.

Cora is in an airplane that is highjacked on its way to Atlanta. The highjacker, a young woman who teaches English in a large city university, orders the pilot to fly to Cuba. In Cuba, Cora falls in love with Castro. They have a big wedding and too many kids to count. Cora is both happy and sad.

Cora is trying to get a part in a play—any play. She stands in line, waiting for a chance to try out for *Peer Gynt.* Nothing happens. She's standing in another line, waiting to try out for *Darkness at Noon.* And another line, for *Little Caesar.* It suddenly occurs to her that *Little Caesar* will be a film and she has had no film experience. Her heart beats faster. She leaves and finds another line. This one, for a 1956 production of *Middle of the Night* at the Shubert Theatre, in New Haven.

Cora has gone away again. She's driving a rented car around a small bay in a foreign country. The sun is going down. It's raining—just a sprinkle. She drives through the mountains where she picks up a hitchhiker. "Oni's my name." Along the same road, another one. She calls herself, "Cathy." And a third, "Eunice." A fourth, "Anita." Huge winds, slamming down from the mountains, nearly push the car off the road into the dale.

Cora is sitting on the edge of the bed, stuffy and hot from the late June afternoon. No air conditioning. I browse her bookshelves for something to read. Would you believe: *Tractatus Logico-Philosophicus* by L. Wittgenstein, *Telepathy and Clairvoyance* by R. Tichner, *The Mentality of Apes* by W. Kohler, *The Psychology of a Musical Prodigy* by G. Revesz, *Metaphysical Foundations of Science* by E. A. Burtt, Ph.D., *Sex and Repression in Savage Society* by B. Malinowski, *Social Life in the Animal World* by F. Alverdes, *How Animals Find Their Way About* by E. Rabund, *The technique of Controversy* by B. B. Bogoslovsky, *History of Chinese Political Thought* by Liang Chi-Chao, *The Trauma of Birth* by

Otto Rank, *The Statistical Method in Economics* by P. S. Florence, *The Art of Interrogation* by E. R. Hamilton, *The Social Life of Monkeys* by S. Zuckerman and *Constitution Types in Delinquency* by W. A. Willemse. No. I know you won't believe it, and she never read any of them but she always meant to. Cora usually meant well. I found nothing I could get into.

But on the coffee table was a copy of *Modern Criminal Investigation* by Harry Söderman and John J. O'Connell. I fingered through its pages and discovered a strange language. None of it came off.

Meanwhile Cora was bitching about the heat.

She was murmuring. ". . . . Happier than I had seen him look before when I kissed him, one, two, three, four times. Playfully, on the nose. . ."

I lifted her eyelids. She was actually sleeping.

I spanked her hip.

Something traumatic clouded the spirit of Canada's face. Then the wisdom of a darkness moved in his eye before he spoke.

"It should bring us closer."

But to this, Cora, listening to him and watching him, could add nothing.

For the first time since the first time, the idea was appealing. What idea. With care it becomes clear. Sometimes it takes a while. But it forms. It builds. It spreads. It becomes useful.

Cora sat facing Canada. Her hands locked behind her. They have just returned from the beach. A crowded polluted day. Canada sucks her earlobes, one at a time. In each there is an embedded blackhead.

With his stern fingers he opened her lips. She refused to react violently to the blunt pressure.

At this point I felt my own mouth open. But I could not remember why I held it open and, meanwhile, Cora's fingers found their way into the area of my external ear. Slowly and with great care, she made tracings.

Cora and Dale together are looking for theatrical work. They try to audition for everything in sight. Even things like *The Little Teacher.*

Canada is home watching old movies on television. There's Edward G. Robinson in *A Lady to Love.* Then Robinson in *The Sea Wolf.* And again in *Confessions of a Nazi Spy.* Again in *The Whole Town's Talking.* Meanwhile it's getting late. With Burt Lancaster, Robinson shows up again in *All My Sons.* Canada is completely submerged in Edward G. Robinson.

When Cora comes in at midnight, Canada has turned into Edward G. Robinson. He's smoking a cigar and wearing a three piece dark gray suit.

Canada has become a drama critic. He's trying to build Cora's career. Right now she's burlesquing in a parody of the current Broadway hit, *The Seagull* by Anton Chekhov. She gets so many curtain calls the clapping echoes back to the seventeenth century. But she's exhausted. After each show Cora goes home and washes the dishes and makes the bed.

She whistles tunes from Gershwin's *Porgy and Bess* and tries
not to argue with Canada.

Canada's dream of God is sexual. Canada and dreams
are sexual, God is sexual. He rams Cora and she says, "Oh,
Canada!"

Canada had always held an interest in sustaining life.
In fact he wanted to become God. As a child he used to say,
"Pip pip." Precisely what he meant by this word he himself
never knew. Nevertheless, he always felt certain that to utter
it influenced the entire universe in its endlessness. Just as
ramming Cora now did.

He always sought ways to improve the world.
However, this urge in Canada was a quality no one except
myself ever noticed and, therefore, naturally, nobody else
appreciated it. Not even the perceptive Cora.

Too often Cora was wrapped up in herself.

When she was like this, it often caused me to forget
incidents or things I felt I should remember. Why, I don't
know. But the inability to recall something would nag me
until I'd have to ask Cora to help me.

Not often but sometimes after a few wild stabs, she
would hit the unseen mark. And, incidentally, it always
worked better when Canada wasn't around.

I really had forgotten what happened to her when she
was out of town. In fact, there was no memory of where
she'd gone nor when it had taken place. Though she had told
me everything. When where and what.

What had taken place Cora now again told me. This
time with an undertone of annoyance.

"Well. You do still remember *why* I left. . . Canada
and I were fucking around, remember. It was the night he

rammed the Coca Cola bottle up my rectum. It was all in fun. We were both drunk. And his thing had given out and I still felt the itch so he used the bottle. Then we went to sleep and the next morning I felt these unbearable cramps all through my stomach and up in my chest. But, you see, I'd no memory of the fact that Canada had accidentally let the bottle slip all the way to a point where he couldn't regain it. So there I was. I couldn't even stand up straight. And that's why I left him. . . ."

"But how did you ever get it out?"

She gave me an intolerable look. Cynically, Cora said, "I consulted a computer."

"Ah, Cora!"

"Well don't ask silly questions! I went to Beth Israel's Emergency Room. They got it out in five minutes. Nothing to it."

"So where did you go when you went away?"

"I was getting to that. You keep interrupting me. I never interrupt you when you're talking. Why you do that?"

"Sorry. Go on."

"I don't think I want to. You've made me mad now. Besides, I told you every detail the day I came back."

I knew from experience it would be pointless to beg her. Cora is the sort of person who cannot be coaxed. I was sitting on a chair near the bed where she sat with her legs crossed, playing with her naked toes. For a moment I considered going over to her and kissing her. Like Canada, taking her breath away. No, that would only increase her annoyance at this point. She has a beautiful heart-shaped mouth I love to kiss. But she's Capricorn, and when you rub a Capricorn the wrong way if you're ever forgiven it is a miracle never to be forgotten.

It isn't that I myself forget their names. The truth is I do not really give a shit about the names these men have who happen to be cops. One might be called *U* and he might be known to copulate with his victims, dead or alive. Another might be known as *A* because he looks like a bull, complete with horns. Still another could be called *D* as a symbol of door or doorway, and, if you like, you might even refer to one as *B,* if somehow you can see how he resembles a house.

But they all continue to come around and the rumor is Canada and I are both very much under suspicion and closely watched. They watch me only because of my involvement with him. I don't believe they would care otherwise. I'm not afraid. I do not even regret my involvement. I couldn't pull away from him now even if I dared doing so.

Anyway I still suspect the law enforcement officers of murdering Cora. Not only was she involved with a militant white group, she was also part of a revolutionary Black group, plus she was branching out into the women's liberation movement. Was a suffragette, but she believed firmly in sexual freedom which, in a way, explains her involvement with Dale. Without any loss of love for Canada and me.

Not that I can live with her attachment to Dale. But still, I refuse to play games. I mean, I can take on Halloween or even Christmas Day. I can handle a day like Labor Day, St. Patrick's Day, even April Fool's Day.

Sometimes I can even handle Canada from the inside out. Other times I must approach him at his edges, and not venture into him too much. He can be very difficult. It is his attitude. *He has an attitude!* He knows Cora is dead yet he has this way of pretending everything is all right and she's very much alive. He invents and reinvents the world as he wishes it to be.

I receive a picture post card. It's from Cora. She's on a

beach somewhere in the Pacific Northwest. There's a man with her. They're holding hands and walking along barefoot. The sand is wet and warm. In about twenty minutes they will be in a cottage arranging roses in a vase. After that they will take a Boeing 707 to Victoria, British Columbia and check into a large room at The Empress where they will stay for five days, sleeping in separate beds. I receive another card. The picture on it shows Cora wearing a delicate taffeta iris colored dress, and smiling. The background is yellow. I draw a blank when I try to remember who the man was.

I draw a picture of Cora. I show it to Canada. "This is a forest covered area, complete with lowlands, rocks, stones, weeds, thunder and lightning, birds and insects." Canada draws a picture of Dale and shows it to me. I say, "This is not a tropical grassland."

I'm a detective trying to solve a murder. No, not a murder. It's a life. Who hired me? I can't face the question.

I'm tailing Cora and Canada and Dale. The three of them are riding together in a gasoline powered 1885 Benz. Ten miles per hour. Canada is driving, I'm walking. It takes them ninety years to reach the theater. The show has closed. The building is no longer there. The Village has changed.

Cora got weak, physically. While she was trying to recover, without becoming bedridden, she never saw Canada's eyes. He kept them behind the darkness of his eyeglasses. And she never pretended anymore, after that first time, that her father was still living. After seeing what sort of effect the trick had on Canada she knew better. The next time he'd probably really get mad. After all, she had long ago broken with her family.

She was like an animal trying to define and patrol her own space. She got sick of looking through commercial magazines, seeing the fashions. The way some girl-boy wanted her to dress.

She wanted to regain the spatial experience of being a child and she worked at it, sometimes. Her unconscious pictorial bias was for *herself* happy alone, walking across grass and under the limbs of trees, harmless animals nearby. She dreamed of it unaware, really, of how far she was from such a life. But unlike "everybody else," Cora was not afraid of her own unconscious life. She believed in the interplay between it and what she saw and felt everyday. Like Canada's dick. Or his face. Or the pots and pans. Or the stove and the kitchen table or the butcher knife which, sometimes, she felt like running through Canada's back.

She still believes in electronic scanners. I can testify to that! She believed in a lot of things and shit that people hadn't gotten around to even thinking about. Stuff like the gentle loving nature of a pure essence called *Odocoileus virginianus*—she claimed it had something to do with wildlife and man's lack of mercy. I don't know. I don't pretend to know. She was into Mother Dependency. Unweaned creatures.

But she was moral as hell, and nothing is more moral than hell except perhaps heaven. Cora didn't believe in killing people. The *idea* of a person, from her point of view, was sacred. Ironic she herself got wasted in such a manner.

But this is not a speech made over a grave. Its nature is

more that of a crossword puzzle or the mood of a mystery novel. In fact I plan to write a mystery novel. Cora would certainly approve of it if I put her in it. This, right here, could be it.

Cora goes to too many parties and she gets drunk too easily. While Canada is drunk, Cora plays around. And that is what leads to fights. What people call good plain dirty fun.

One night I kissed naked Cora in a musty hallway when she was trying to squat. For some reason. I couldn't believe she really was that tired.

They found some of her teeth near the window.

And the police department plays it up big. They bring out their gadgets and hook them up to whatever they want to inspect. Even hook them up to people.

"Give me the spoon."

"I don't have it."

"Fingerprint the neighbors."

"Why?"

"You heard me."

"Here. Put the silicone beneath the skin. The prints turn out better. Inject it."

"It's dark in here. . . ."

"Go out to the car. Get the ultraviolet ink."

"Your mother."

One young man was wearing rubber gloves and was picking his teeth with a dirty toothpick.

Dry blood was being wiped out on narrow sheets of paper. My thoughts: these motherfuckers care nothing for Cora and they automatically think Canada or I killed her. Fuck 'em.

They had already drawn a circle around the large area where the disaster took place. And one was sprinkling white powder within that area. Also there were the shattered pieces of a suitcase.

The whole scene made me want to leave.

Canada and I leave town. It's not easy. In Maryland, we get work operating a crane on a construction site. Lifting a hundred and forty tons of mashed potatoes from a vacant lot to another vacant lot. Pay? Fifty cents and a fish sandwich. For spending change, we stick up a mail train, swooping with seven million, which lasts us a few days. We live it up in Winnemucca, Nevada; dance with buckeyed Indians in Pierce, Idaho; do the fox-trot with hippies in Eugene, Oregon; backtracking, we hide out in Swiftbird, South Dakota, where a fella with alert, gentle eyes and red hair, helps us invent new identities. With our new cards, we return East, dressed as limbo dancers, with the false endorsement of Teresa Marquis of the Island of St. Lucia, we get work at the Palace Theatre and Carnegie Hall. We're a smash success. Our manager, a bird-watcher from Dwaarkill, New York, book us for a tour of Italy. But by now we're exhausted. We separate.

So I moved on to another place, a place more intense. Not that *I* necessarily wanted more drama. Canada is the one who likes drama. He tries to burst and he tries to crack.

Sometimes Canada thinks himself a sledgehammer. What can you do with a person like that. You certainly cannot go on evading him. He is not that kind of spirit.

To keep my mind off the problems of Cora's death, I watch television. It slushes back and forth before me. In the afternoon TV is dull shit and it lodges you in its dullness; yet it gives you a weird vegetable sort of copout security.

Sometimes Canada comes into the same room and watches too. But he's usually too impatient to sit for long. It's too unreal, he says. They keep showing the same old movies. Mrs. Webb, again, is reminded that someone is at the door to see her.

Anyway Canada suddenly stands up and, leaving the room, screams Cora's name.

In the hallway, I hear him shout: "I can smell her beautiful musty armpits!"

Obviously, he refuses to accept her sudden death. I understand. I am in the same boat.

Cora, with her teddybear, plays inside a boat. She tickles her clit with the soft arm of the toy. She feels a pleasant and annoying restlessness. A boy in a washed out green cotton shirt wanders down to the edge of the water. He stands watching her and she does not stop. He has his hands crammed into his tight pockets. Playing pocket pool. His eyes reflect a muddy yellow light and he seems angry or afraid.

And Cora understood anger and fear without thinking about such qualities. She understood her understanding and she noticed the boy trying to see under her skirt. She understood that too.

But now she throws her teddybear in the water and looks toward the orange sunset. And the boy runs his hand under her skirt. Or is it a dress. I can't see too clearly. I see very dimly in the sunset. Or is it a sunrise.

I have only a certain vision and my thoughts play too frequently in Cora's footsteps. The way her feet fall, the sounds left by her walking. She perhaps will never overcome the facts of her crucial moments.

Canada plays tricks on Cora and she adjusts to his tricks. The action is no big thing. She is soft texture and quivering flesh, and she is a person too. But Canada has trouble. Sometimes it is troublesome for him to see this. He sees the television screen but he cannot always see the street below their window, or how Cora opens nor the furniture they got from the flea market or himself from the bathroom mirror. But he means well and often he means to be very good.

He glides his tongue along the edges of Cora's hairline. And I watch from the far side of the dim room. The soft splash of wet vehicles going by outside.

"The living tissue," Cora says.

"Are you pregnant?"

"No, Canada. I'm desperate. I feel tense and desperate." She turns away toward the wall.

I walk closer to see better and the afternoon sunlight touches my face, causing me to retreat.

I hide in the kitchen but do not look at the rubber plants. In here there is no sunlight. But I hear the French horns again and children outside screaming.

In the front Canada and Cora are laughing together. I feel they are probably laughing at me.

I open the silverware drawer again, just to make sure

the loaded pistol is still there. Canada might have taken it away, for security—which he shall never have. But it is still in its place in the drawer.

I hate to say each thing has its place but that is the way this house is run. Cora runs this house and she is quite regular. She regulates everything her own way. But I've gotten used to it and it doesn't bother me so much anymore.

I'll take the gun into the front room and threaten to kill them both if they don't stop laughing. I will tell them that, and if they don't stop, I'll really do it. I think I'll do it. I hope I *can* do it. I don't really know if I should do it but, perhaps, if I start by lifting the weapon and walking away toward the front with it in my hand, the reason for doing it might suddenly develop. Right now, I know no reason. I have no reason. My thoughts are the kind people keep to themselves. Like the fear of dying and everybody's endless quiet desperation.

I'm at the last outport. The nearest seaport is a hundred miles downstream. I'm waiting for Cora's next move.

Canada comes from the woods into the clearing. He's wearing overalls. Carrying a shotgun. He squints watching me closely. His mouth opens but he says nothing.

I make up a name. "I'm Dick James." I think fast. "My boat got a leak." I think even faster. "It floated off downstream."

Cora likes to be alone. She shoots live movies, make

up mystery plays, melodramas, does frame by frame animations of her own visions. She's alone in her apartment looking in the mirror. Boris Karloff looks back at her. She smiles at him. Behind her, Peter Lorre murmurs something about being cautious. A tree frog is sitting on her dresser. Cora does a turnabout and sees Charlie Chaplin and W. C. Fields standing in the doorway.

Cora, light-stepping on her toes, goes outside and stands at the side of her doorway, looking away into nothing. I see the soft purple shadows on the other side of her. Her eyelids flutter and she lifts her right hand, extends it, reaching for nothing. Across the street is a huge billboard. On it SEND NO MONEY. But she cannot see the small print from this distance. The city, all around her. The space around her. She wonders about the mountains. The forest. The desert. The sea.

So standing here in her own doorway, she waits for her lover, Dale. She needs variety, still a child at heart, still dreaming of the prince who won't ever come. But she keeps trying to come back to herself.

When she sees Dale she will not make a move. Cora moves only after Dale has entered the house agreed on. It is their meeting place lately. They never go into it together. One at a time is safest. Prior to meetings telephone arrangements are made. And never more than an hour or so ahead of time. 'Cause anything can happen. Changes. Interruptions. She likes Dale and doesn't want to lose him. Neither does she want to lose herself. Nor Canada, nor me.

She prefers Canada to watch me so he won't have time to keep an eye on her.

Once Dale has gone into the building (from sight), she moves. She goes slowly across the street, swaying her wide hips, her high ass churning. She is examining her fingernails as she moves.

Once she gains the opposite side of the street, without picking up speed, Cora starts along the sidewalk in the direction of the house where Dale waits for her.

When she is directly across from the house, she returns to the side she started from, and, without being too obvious about it, looks all around at the windows of the houses, and, up and down the street. She also looks up at the sky. Seeing all is clear and already feeling the beginning of an orgasm, she walks swiftly up the walkway, climbs the steps, opens the unlocked door, enters, closes it behind herself, locks it and stands still. Listening for him.

Rich and famous now, Cora is at a fancy party rubbing shoulders with Gina Lollobrigida, Alfred Hitchcock, Shirley MacLaine, Bing Crosby and Clark Gable. Cora feels especially charming until a salamander mudpuppy jumps out of her dress, coming from the space between her breasts. Joan Crawford lifts her eyebrows. James Dean smiles, a sly sneaky smile. Lon Chaney coughs and says he must leave. At this point, a spadefoot toad and a Texas hook-nosed snake fall from under Cora's dress.

Standing inside a house usually brings back to Cora the fact that she had never actually been inside the house she wanted to live in, spend her time in, sleep in, eat in, fuck in, dream in, love in. Such a house might have a barn nearby and the whole place might have a Gallic accent. You might find it somewhere in a remote area of Westchester County or in New

London, Connecticut. Her furniture would be antique and always highly polished. Her settee would be covered with a modest though colorful tapestry. Good prints in frames on the walls. Rafters above the fireplace in the cool, wide living room. Cora could easily imagine all of it, but, for me, I could see only the white cabinets over the kitchen sink. And in one of the drawers near the stove, a pistol, loaded. And I remain aware of its presence like someone who, because he possesses it, must somehow eventually *use* the weapon.

Often Cora tries to invest Dale with her own vision of the house, with herself in it, in the kitchen. She sees herself standing at the sink with an apron tied around her naked body and Dale approaching her from behind. He has just come home from his job where he is happy, where he is boss. No. That's Dale's vision. Cora erases it and replaces it with her own: she's at the sink, but she's fully dressed. In fact she's wearing a long, elegant, cardigan evening gown that clings to her lovely figure. It is silver and it shimmers. Its edges are in greige jersey and the buttons are glowing silver balls. Her feet are clad in sandals and her hair is pulled tightly back into a bun, and it sparkles beneath the kitchen light. She is making supper for her man who will soon arrive. His face isn't quite clear in her mind yet. As she dips the wet pieces of chicken into a powdery substance, Cora tries to make the face of her man come into focus. But it continues to elude her as she puts the chicken, one piece at a time, into the hot bubbling oil in the frying pan on the stove. Suddenly a bubble of grease bursts wildly against her hands and arms and up into her face, and she screams as her skin begins to peel.

She realizes she must not confine herself to the kitchen. It is too singular an image. Cora is aware that she has many other sides. She is not simply a thing to stand in a kitchen just as she is not simply a creature whose mission in life is to receive her man's orgasm or ejaculation—whichever the case may be. She has many dispositions, she has a round shape, her spirit is round her eyes, her arms and her legs. She moves around and around. Cora moves up and down the spirit of her coiling self. She has an endless meaning. Even as Canada fucks Cora, Cora fucks Canada.

"Do you feel it?"

The fact that Dale really has little or no character doesn't help matters. I cannot help him if he refuses to focus. How can I be blamed for his lack of seriousness. And it isn't that he doesn't talk to me. He talks too much to me, really, and he plots too much, has too many secrets, leaves nothing in the open. Whatever it was about him that attracted Cora shall always remain a mystery to me. Anyone who'd choose to make her dream chandelier from the worn-out wheel of a farm manure spreader has to be strange. Cora *was* strange.

And she remains as weird as ever. I go through the things she left trying to understand *why* she owned this or that. What it might have meant to her.

Cora is teaching Canada the Charleston. He can't get the hang of it. He keeps doing a Nijinsky ballet step. In despair, Cora sits in a corner playing with an alligator lizard she got from the pet shop. The lizard says, "Burp." The phone rings. It's long distance from Russia. They want Cora to star in a production at the Maly. As she dresses, Canada throws a dozen eggs at her. An hour later she's flying to Russia. The airplane crashes. She dies. Canada, who was secretly the pilot, gets fifty years in the penitentiary. In the pen, a thug named Dale, in for life, teaches Canada to do the Charleston.

Canada believes in lists. He makes up a list of things he thinks he might need. Even demolition weapons. You never know. Fifty shells of TNT; two hundred units of dynamite; four caps of tear gas; fifty hand grenades. However a list of the stuff was not the same as having the items. When he read the words, speaking them to himself, they came closer to being the items themselves than the scribble—since the scribble itself had already achieved an entity, a concreteness, an independence.

He also owned a pistol and a shotgun. Arm yourself or harm yourself. Uncle Sam is watching you. Self-defense is the first law of natural law.

But Canada never talked about his possessions. Especially not about his weapons. The possession of most of them in New York was "illegal." That of course was purely technical.

The day Cora was murdered, Canada checked his supply of weapons. It was early morning and he simply looked into the closet where he kept the stuff. Nothing more rigid than a casual check.

Later he went downstairs to make a phone call.

"I have a list of equipment I need to show you."

The person on the other end said to Canada, "Did you know I was thinking about your goods."

He waited.

"As a matter of fact," the voice went on, "I just got a call a few minutes ago. Somebody wanted to know how we were set . . . . "

"Did you tell?"

"How could I."

Canada dragged the last of a roach.

"Can you come over, Canada?"

"What time?"

"I have no clock. Does it matter?"

"Cora went to the laundry to drop off some sheets."

"So?"

"Can you come over here?"

"This is silly, Canada. Of course not."

A buzzing replaced the space where the voice might have again sounded. And since buzzing amounts to a dead line, he quickly hung up. He felt chills, hot ones.

He went to the closet and looked at his hats, shoes, shirts, trousers and gloves. Yes, they *looked like* him. He then examined Cora's stuff: slacks, dresses, blouses, skirts, shoes, even her hose. There wasn't as much of her in these as there was of him in his.

Now, in grand coolness, he moved from the spot before the closet to the area of the window. Outside, through the brisk wind, two lovely girls walked side by side. One in red, the other in blue. Soft colors, soft girls. (Maybe.) Canada felt an unwelcomed buildup of tears behind the surface of his face. *One of those girls in Cora.* But this didn't last. Though the one he now focused on walked like Cora it was, for him, a self-defeating trick played by himself on himself. *But O God that terrible sweet gait!* And tears finally oozed from the rims of his eyes. While behind him the phone was blasting.

When Canada picked up the receiver he was stabbed in the ear by a buzzing tone. As he hung up he tried to fight his awareness of a huge sense of pain. *Why am I so depressed.*

Now. He was on the phone again. The voice asked him: "Why are you so depressed, Canada?" The question seemed purely rhetorical. As he listened to the question, Canada was also aware of not listening for whom the voice belonged to.

One thing was clear: he still possessed the powerful will that enables one to hang up the phone. So he did. The phone had lately been an annoying ugly instrument anyway. Crank calls in the stillness of night, nightmare emptiness screaming on the other end, the unborn or dead waking him, warning him . . .

Cora is never defeated. Even when depressed, she goes out looking for parts in plays. Stands in audition lines three miles long. She meets a lot of interesting people this way. In alphabetical order, she has met: Albee, Edward; Albert, Edward; Allen, Gracie; Ball, Lucille; Bogart, Humphrey; Brown, Clarence; Calloway, Cab; Crist, Judith; Daley, James; Day, Doris; Douglas, Kirk; Garfield, John; Hopper, Hedda; Hutton, Betty; Jolson, Al; Kael, Pauline; Kelly, Gene; Lee, Gypsy Rose; Lupino, Ida; MacLaine, Shirley; Mussolini, Benito; and Torn, Rip.

Louella Parsons is interviewing Cora Hull. Question: Will NBC-TV release that hush-hush film they have in which you are outdoing Linda Lovelace? Answer: *Sheathlike* is a scientific movie about crime on the streets of our major cities. I play the part of a supercop who can kick the asses of sixty-six thousand men in the blink of an eye. Louella Parsons: But I've been informed that it's a *sex* movie! Cora: It is, indeed *it is*!

Canada is a cop again. He's out arresting junkies and thugs. Off duty, he stops in a bar. Sitting at the bar is a man who might be Dillinger. The woman with him looks like Anna Sage, the woman in red. The bartender could easily be Lucky Luciano. Over the bar is a pointing by Thomas Hart Benton. There's a television set on a platform attached to the wall.

It's on. It's the news, showing an earthquake killing three thousand people at that very minute somewhere. Canada orders a beer.

After they all cleared out I went in and measured the space her body had occupied. Figured I knew her contour a little better than the police doctor.

Sorry now that I stopped her from coming around. Yet I shouldn't be. We continued to see each other. Didn't like her nosy landlady, such a snobbish bitch! Always wondered if she was going to tell Canada of my little visits while he was out. Guess she never did.

But we often wondered what would happen.

"He'd kill us both."

She got up and came to my side, kissed me. At that moment Canada came in. I cleared my throat and closed my eyes. I waited for his reaction but he said nothing. I looked at Cora and she too was hung in a long silence.

Canada comes home and finds the rubber plant doing the dishes. Cora is reading a book about Jerome Kern.

A blind snake is curled in the middle of the floor.

Rita Haywood is screaming in the room. Canada looks around. Oh. The television.

Later that night, Canada does a transatlantic lindy hop from Europe to the states and landing in a courtroom in the South, he accidentally gets sentenced to the penitentiary as one of the Scottsboro boys.

Canada told the kid to go away. "Go fuck off, son."

But it wasn't jealousy, see. The point was the kid was taking up too much of Cora's time. Canada would come home and there was the kid sitting there, nice and cozy with Cora, like she was his mama or something. At first I didn't get the point. Also, at first, my reaction to Canada's attitude was negative. How could a grown man in all fairness tell a kid to go fuck off. But he had a way of letting his pain out on others. And this time he'd just come in from a fight. A bad terrible fight he'd won. Which for him was worse than losing. But the boy, you could see, tried desperately not to cry. He wiped the string of snot hanging from his nose on the sleeve of his green shirt. I watched the kid's top teeth nibble at his bottom lip until the flesh turned blue-red.

After the boy left Canada spoke defensively. "Kid hanging around all the time, he might steal something. Little snottynose sonofabitch!"

Cora pulled her open robe together across her naked stomach and looked toward the kitchen. Where the gun was in the drawer.

"He hasn't taken anything, Canada."

"How do you know?"

"Nothing's missing."

I have a terrible time understanding precisely what goes on between them and myself. It is extremely hard work. I try to see how they speak to each other and listen to their words, but they keep tricking me. All I feel I can successfully do is *look* at Cora. Fill my senses with her loveliness. She is just there. I'd try to force her to do anything. Yet I force her all the time. I keep annoying her, trying to get her to open to me, really reveal herself. The split trunk of a tree. Her spit drips on my neck.

Dear Cora, I'm sending you James Moody of Savannah, Georgia, and Savannah Churchill of New Orleans and Brooklyn. Their music will hold your hand gently. Be sure to see *The Thief of Baghdad*, silent film, not solely for Douglas Fairbanks. Watch Jesse Fuller too. Listen to "Night Train." See Ella in *Pete Kelley's Blues*. You have to go back to 1955. Play Lady Day. Dig on Sister Rosetta Tharpe. Yours sincerely, C.

Cora stands in line waiting to try out for Road Runner in a new comedy by a young playwright who looks like J. Edgar Hoover. A soft-shelled turtle falls from Cora's purse. Everybody in line falls over laughing. A dozen patch-nosed snakes begin coming out of the woodwork. The director, who looks like Frederic March, comes running down the hallway, waving his arms wildly. "Get out while you can!" Vine snakes, worm snakes, yellow-lipped snakes, and boas too are coming, moving around and between the legs of the young actors and actresses as they run, screaming.

In her Fouke-dyed black fur seal coat, Cora is ready to go to the theater for her rehearsal. I am on the bed resting. Watching her hesitation. She has trouble saying goodbye. It's part of her charm.

"I don't want to leave. I can't say goodbye to you . . . ."

She kisses me quickly. My eyes take a dolly shot of her rushing from the room. The hallway door banging behind her.

I wake up cautiously. The day has to go well, so care must be taken. Otherwise by noon everything will be fucked up and my head will be definitely *outtolunch*! So I walk slowly from the bedroom into the kitchen. When the coffee is ready I drink it very slowly, carefully. The slightest thing can ruin everything. Except Cora. Even if she calls early in the morning, breaking my sleep, she remains exempt from the pattern of people and things able to ruin my day. So each moment is a fundamental moment.

"Don't worry. Everything will be fine."

Cora is at another theatrical party. She's talking with a famous Negro writer. He's grinning and acting very pompous. Cora can't believe this creature is the author of a book she enjoyed so much. The man is in his sixties and he's wearing a pin-striped suit. He chuckles a lot between sentences. The sentences themselves don't seem to mean much. After all, he's talking to a woman. A lady. Cora is annoyed.

The next day they make a movie from his novel and Cora stars in it. Dale has the male lead. Cora and Dale are dirt farmers in the South. They do everything but fuck. They steal chickens and read science fiction novels by brilliant writers like Chop Belany. The white folks get angry and threaten to burn their house down and run them into the woods. But Dale and Cora hold their own. They have a stack of rocks behind the front door; they will fight till the end.

Cora is away being interviewed by Cecil B. DeMille. I'm here, on the bed, thinking about my future. I want to blur the distinctions between it and the past. I'll make up everything from now on. If I want a commercial airline to crash with Cora and Dale on it doing it in the dark, I'll do that. Or have them go down at sea in a steamer caught in a violent typhoon near Iceland, or in an exploration vessel off the West Indies. I'll do anything I like. I'm extending reality, not retelling it.

I find everything I touch falling to pieces, and the pieces themselves continue to break into smaller and smaller segments. Cora, who enjoys unusual conditions, considers this one. When I mention my misfortune to her the crisp edge in her voice always drops. She knows how to be very cynical. She's eight years younger than me and she teases me about my age. I try to get her to understand that it is not a joke: I do feel old and I have made peace with getting old. Though I am still trying to come to terms with dying. Between my own words, the tip of her tongue touches the dry area inside my left ear.

"Be nice."

As she walks away I am consumed by the swaying motion of her high ass. Carefree elegance and fluffy thick black hair bouncing on her shoulders.

I can only hope that Cora herself, when touched by my hands, will not fall to pieces.

I cut another notch into the totem pole of my own life and pretend that someone else does it. My modesty is simply another form of arrogance. I erase what I say if it isn't "nice."

Cora, reading the xeroxed copy of *Hades* paces across the room and continues to murmur to herself. She's serious about learning her part. I hope she makes it. Canada may not like the idea of Cora on stage kissing other men but I feel it's good for her—it's an outlet. The pressure won't build that way. Her interest in acting evens off my drunk spirit, and helps me forgive her for her flirting. But who the fuck am I to feel cocky enough to forgive her for anything. I have no right and she doesn't belong to anyone—not even herself. She's still whispering the script to herself. As far as she's concerned, I'm not in the room.

So I go to the mirror and study my own terrible face. There is a very soft tapping on the door.

"Yes?"

Dale dresses as Ava Gardner. But I'm not fooled. He tries to get a part in a melodrama on Broadway. It doesn't work.

It's snowing outside. I'm in here making this novel. A whistling tree frog on the arm of the armchair, watches a coachwhip snake moving along the floor. On the wall is an Edward Hopper painting of an all-night diner. The loneliness kills me. They bury me in Atlanta. Cora invites Shirley MacLaine and Marcello Mastroianni to the funeral but they don't show. A lot of colored writers send flowers.

No matter how hard I try I can't make Dale's face focus. I guess because I dislike him. Hate him. Jealous of him maybe. Who knows. Maybe his face isn't the kind of face that focuses well. Some do, others don't. But I really suspect I've blocked him . . . .

Because Cora kisses Dale's neck—because they obviously get together and fuck like wild animals. Such acts break down my will to communicate. I lose faith in the key. And I begin to dislike kissing.

Cora means too much to me.

"Say it a number of times. Watch what happens. The idea begins to break."

"Cora means too much to me."

Again.

Canada I respect. And he too means much, very much, to me. Though he tends to be crude, I still hold him close to my skin. I touch him and that is something most people cannot do. Even when he has terrible nights, sleepless nights, when he dreams of the godless world where he is an aimless victim.

Canada wrapped wet towels around the broken pieces of glass. Who broke the bottles on Cora's clean floor I can't say. I don't know. Canada certainly didn't break them. I didn't break them.

Canada has to find a way to relax. He sends for Red Garland to play piano. The sunlight comes in through the window showing thousands of kiwis on the wallpaper pecking in New Zealand sand. Stan Getz follows Red. With a funky ballad. The tenor sax is an act of love. Canada closes his eyes. He's back in 1938 listening to Ella sing, "A-tisket, A-tasket."

He's better. But it's raining.

I'm caught in the rain. My umbrella flies away. A picture of James Mason washes from a wall to the sidewalk. A commercial airliner crashes in front of me. Cora steps out of the rubble and starts crying. I try to console her. She says, "It's no use."

At her place, we discuss the possibility of throwing a big party to celebrate nothing. We'll invite Picasso, Grant Wood, Duke Ellington, Isadora Duncan and Stalin. They should get along. The idea of the party makes us happy. We start doing the Twist.

Lately I've had to stop too many times. Because I lack examples. I still possess the spirit of Cora and I understand Canada, his moods and his deeds. I keep stopping to try to find out where I am.

Cora came back into the room with a Coke bottle. In it was a liquid, certainly not soda pop. She sat in a chair near the bed and, holding the bottle in her left hand, deliberately shook the bottle and watched the liquid foam. From the bed I watch her lovely heart-shaped mouth. Maybe I should get up, go across the room and kiss it. I love kissing it. The soft flesh gives beneath my pressure. She reaches for me, touches me in my most private and most tender places at such moments. I sink into her. Often I forget my own name. I can't pull away from her now.

"What's in the bottle?"

"I don't believe you really care."

"But I continue to ask . . . "

"Do you know Dale?"

"Don't avoid my question. Is there some sort of plot against you?"

"Sometimes," Cora says, "I can handle you *and* Canada. Usually, however, I have to approach both of you at your edges. I have as much trouble with you two as I have with myself."

Suddenly she threw the bottle on the floor and, as she started taking the hairpins from her tightly woven hair, I watched, with one eye, the liquid drip out onto the red Indian rug.

Outside fingernails are clawing at the door.

For kicks Cora and I go to see *Gone With the Wind*. But something is wrong. It's about the Lindberghs trying to escape the swift G-men of the FBI. Suddenly it changes. It's about World War I. A scene where tiny bombers are dropping bombs on thousands of babies in cribs. We leave the theater. The screen follows us. It moves along a few yards ahead, still showing the same movie. The scenes keep changing. A million people are wiped out in a snow storm. A policeman stops us. We're arrested.

Cora, using the stub of what was once a long yellow pencil, now wrote carefully on the blue line of a yellow notepad sheet: Maiden (*Greek*). She herself understood it. If no one else ever would.

Then. Thinking gently of the cheeks of Dale's ass, she wrote beneath those two words: Valley (*Anglo-Saxon*).

She spends a lot of time trying to explain electronic scanners to me. Not knowing that. I care less than a fuck. I can testify to nothing she says. Cora often talks too much. Tends to be filled with verbal fury. She also tends to rant. When I do not check her. Caution her. Anyway I have absolutely no interest in electronic scanners. I care about them about as much as I care about speech-making. Or the ritual that goes on around a grave after someone has been buried.

"You should read mystery novels. Keep yourself busy. Take your mind off yourself."

Cora laughs. "This is too much."

"You go to too many parties. You should read books *about* mystery novels, Cora."

"You should be at my wedding reception."

"Cora, you should rest."

"Canada," she says, "he will find my teeth near a window in a vacant house. I dreamed that he did. And everywhere photographers were snapping pictures."

"Baby," I said, "you think about yourself too much."

"Death," she said.

"Cora. Cora, think of life. Not death. Think of the terrible loveliness right here *now*!"

"Or what we don't have. Spoons. Gadgets and hooks. I think of things and I think of myself."

"Yourself too much."

"You stay quiet in me. I speak in myself. I am equal. I treat you as well as I treat Canada or Dale. *You.*"

"I don't have you."

"You."

"You have my fingerprints."

"The police."

"The cops. What do they know about anything."

"What is this you're writing on the notepad?"

"Looks like blood stains."

"You always make me want to go away."

"Make me," she said.

"Your suitcase, Cora. For example."

"I need things, motherfucker."

Cora was never a mother. Though she was pregnant several times. Each time she lost the thing before the fourth month. Her womb was slightly tilted to the left. Also there were the shattered pieces of her self to deal with.

Cora is in *Hell and Frisco Bay*. She has the part Fay Wrey was supposed to have. Something has gone wrong. Cora is the understudy. Alan Ladd is standing on a stool; he is kissing Jayne Mansfield. Director, Frank Tuttle, is upset. This is not the way . . . .

Cora is in *The Cincinnati Kid*. She is trying to pass herself off as Cab Calloway's daughter. Steve McQueen couldn't care less. Cora does a few jazz steps, they look like ballet steps. Calloway is not impressed. Karl Malden scratches his nose, blinks his eyes. He looks at Cora. And he says, "You all right, kid!"

Cora is in *The House of Strangers* with Susan Haywood. Twentieth Century Fox is paying Cora a million dollars a day. All she has to do is become Susan Haywood so the real Susan Haywood can take a break.

Cora says, "This book you're writing isn't nearly as strange as reality. The only way you're going to make any sense is to stick with the impossible. Any resemblance to the past or present should be purely accidental."

We're in bed fucking. I'm not in the mood for what she's saying. I have her legs wide and I'm rolling smoothly between them.

"You'll have to keep making up the most impossible events you can think of to hold my interest. Oh yes! Fuck me, fuck me!"

I watch television but it does not keep my mind off the fact that Cora is dead. She might have been alive. Anybody who is dead might still be alive. It depends. Yet it does not lodge.'

Nothing changes. Yet everything must change. Cora changes before your natural eye. Everything about Cora is constantly changing. Not only does her life depend on it. But mine does too. Canada's life depends on Cora's changes. Dale's hangups depend on what she does.

It is a *long* story.

"Too many stories are too long," Cora tells me.

"Fuck you!" I suddenly say.

And hearing the anger in my voice, she suddenly realizes that I am pissed. And from this point on she knows how to cool it. She finds a mystery book to read.

The mystery turns out to be a story about the end of the world written by a group of scientists who survived The Holocaust. The scientists spend all their time making concrete poetry and reading it on tape. They play these tapes for each other when they're drunk late at night. When they are all very, very drunk, they order a large cake from the local bakery. Always there is a woman hidden in it. At the high point of the party, the woman jumps out of the cake and shakes her naked ass and tits all over the place, in their faces. They love it. On one such occasion, the woman is Cora. When she shakes her tits in their faces, their faces fall off. When she shakes her ass in their faces, their teeth fall out.

Cora is reading about herself in this continuous mystery. She's trying to make all the mysterious ends meet. At the same time, she is trying to escape . . . .

Canada and Cora catch Gerry Mulligan on baritone sax doing "Venus De Milo."

Cora is in a lumber yard. Musicians are coming out of the woodwork. Clarinets piano vibes trumpets tenor sax trombone drums are speaking a language that rhymes.

Next door, two thugs are kidnapping the daughter of a

rich thug. We can hear the racket. We can also hear an express train moving through their living room. The train is full of G-men and bigamists. The child is screaming as the thugs escape with her down the back stairway. Neighbors lay low.

I turn on the news. A thug is hijacking an airplane. He's demanding that the pilot fly to Cuba.

I give up. In the kitchen I eat a huge ice cream sundae.

"These are the same old movies. Mrs. Webb, again."

"No, Cora. This is a thing on how to use jigs as electrodes. What you're witnessing right now is the commercial."

She goes across the room and turns the set off. "The fucking screen slushes back and forth in my head too much. They keep showing the same old shit. And I refuse to copout this way."

"Why are you all dressed up?"

"Because I'm impatient. What's your name anyway?"

"Yes."

"Endless bullshit. Misdirected technology."

"Bullshit. Bullshit, Cora."

"Well. It's fine with me. Whatever you do."

"It gives you a weird sensation."

"It's too unreal. Vegetable like."

"Canada," Cora says, "*now.*"

"How is he?"

"You fuck his wife. That's how he is." She lit a long well-packed cigarette. Scratched her hip. Looking out the window. "Was that someone at the door?"

"It reminds me of someone."

"This morning Canada had the TV on at seven. Some program about the technique of Kiss-Roll Coating. Plastics. He has a mechanical mind. Did you know?"

"Polyester resins."

"Canada is my baby, though. My sledgehammer!"

"I'm jealous. So I might move to another place."

"You won't. You can't. It slushes back and forth in your skull. You can't keep your mind off me. My cunt has you by the balls." And she laughs.

Someone knocks at the door.

Cora puts a finger to her mouth. Could it be the sunrise. Or the edge of the water.

I make a motion to answer, to move toward the door. Cora shakes her pretty head. She whispers, "It's the boy in the green cotton shirt. Don't answer it. I feel musty and I am sick of the orange sunset that comes in when I open the door for him. He'll go away. Just be cool."

But the knocking continues, and I think of Poe and I think of Cora's orange sunset and her teddybear. I remember how she spoke to Canada: "I feel tense and desperate."

I tiptoe closer to her.

The knocking goes away, and I go to the kitchen and look at the dying rubber plants.

When I return Cora, breathing deeply, rests in the chair from the flea market.

"Canada is in trouble," she says.

"Why?"

"He's been away for . . . crucial moments. This time with a difference and . . . distance between us, real, and there is a space between our different intentions."

"You sound on the far side of a dim room." I took a notebook from my pocket and wrote with a ballpoint pen: "Cora is a mixing-vessel." Then I looked at her nervous twitching face. "Are you pregnant?"

"No. I'm desperate. I want to count the silverware or even polish it. Anything to take my mind off myself. I like to have everything in its place. I like regulating everything. I like to keep records. I insist on *order*."

"All right."

"Listen. I have a headache. Why don't you go."

I feel crushed as I walk by the billboard that says: SEND NO MONEY. All around me is terror and in it people move.

An hour later I called her. Never was able to adjust to her voice through the phone.

"Listen," Cora said.

"Cora."

"Now, now." Heavy breathing.

Tongue clicking against teeth. "Cora, Cora."

Cora answers the phone. "This is a recording: You are out to lunch. This is a recording: You are out to lunch. This is a recording: You are out to lunch."

Cora is on Eighth Street. A young white woman, selling communist newspapers, attacks her. Throws her down. Straddles her. Crams all the newspapers down Cora's throat. They cause her to shit all day for days.

The phone is ringing. I answer it. "Is Eli Bolton there?"

"You have the wrong number. No Bolton here."

The phone rings again. "Is Moses Westby there?"

"Sorry. No Westby here."

Cora places a stack of records on the record player. For years she listens to Buck Clayton, Thelonious Monk, Bix Beiderbecke, Benny Carter, Hoagy Carmichael, Chico Hamilton. They drench her. She sleeps with the records, dances through the music.

I want this book to be anything it wants to be. A penal camp. A bad check. A criminal organization. A swindle. A prison. Devil's Island. I want the mystery of this book to be an absolute mystery. Let it forge its own way into the art of deep sea diving. Let it walk. I want it to run and dance. And be sad. And score in the major league all-time records. I want it to smoke and drink and do other things bad for its health. This book can be anything it has a mind to be.

On the porch along the rail are blue and pink flowers. When Cora came out on her toes and stood to one side of the doorway, she didn't notice them. She never noticed them and they had been there for ages. One side of her face soon became blue shade. Earlier it might have been purple. Funny for an apartment building here in the city to have a porch like this. Like in some small hick town. There are objects that force her to wander around and between things. Anyway she does not want to seem too obvious. She tends to be uptight about going to the empty house. She has this feeling that EYES everywhere are watching her movements. Spies. Canada has *paid spies* watching, checking her activities.

I shouldn't spend time and energy trying to understand and explain anybody. I should spend time in myself. Or in Canada, looking out through his eyes. Try to do something useful from his point of view. I could get a fresh look at Cora maybe. Or from Dale's particular vantage point. If I could just focus him. He certainly is more than just *Dale*; Dale has to be a human being who is not simply Cora's lover. After all I'm Cora's lover too. And Canada, in a way, could be said to be Cora's lover as well. He probably loves her as well as any of her lovers ever loved her. But I like to imagine she has never before been involved with any other men except the ones I'm aware of: Canada, Dale, myself. I can handle myself to a degree. I can deal with Canada most of the time. Dale, I'm coming to terms with him. It takes time. Nothing about Cora is simple.

I keep hoping I'll wake up and be relieved that this is simply a dream. I really would not want to wake up though. I say a lot of things I don't really mean and, too often, I get away with them. But dreaming isn't all that different from living. This is what *I* understand, and it is what I have so much trouble trying to show Cora. She pretends she doesn't understand. But I have faith, and I do get a sort of release from tension when I have to deal with her and her problems. I don't like always being involved with her and the shit she's always in. I really don't. And I do mean it this time.

I turn on the television set. *I Love Lucy*.
"It's corny."
"I thought you liked the show, Cora."
"I've changed. I'm back to reality."
"You talk shit, baby."
"Fuck you, man."

I walk across the grass. From this angle I see Cora standing in the doorway. The other side of her face. The light shines on this side. She needs variety. I need the variety she gets. In her hand she holds a book. Something about her presence here seems too mysterious. What is Cora up to. Would you believe this quiet girl is the same person who danced in beer halls and kicked up a storm in civil rights marches.

I walk to the other side of the porch to see her from still another angle. The curve of her full mouth. The time she went to that weird party decked out as a mermaid. I'll never forget it. Hard to believe. Her face is in shadows on this side. Lately she can't remember her dreams. But she has them every night. I hear her murmuring in her sleep when she dozes at my place. I don't like her from this side as well as from the front.

I stand in front of her and she smiles. I can imagine how she looks beneath her stylish red dress. Red shoes. A red ribbon in her dark thick hair. I can see in my mind her soft mound, the lips damp and slighly puffy. She needs variety. She still dreams, daydreams. She thinks of the terrible prince from her childhood and she seeks him. What can I do. I can't tell her: you're wasting your time. I'd drive her farther from me. I can't afford that. I'm already barely hanging on to her. Please, Cora, come back to my reality. Start a new way.

I keep struggling with her fingers. Trying to understand their connections. I struggle my way through my own dreams. I don't analyze them anymore. I never did it very well anyway. Often her efforts leave her where she starts. Even in my dreams. I keep trying to force her hands open to see what she's hiding. She has nothing in them, yet I know she's concealing something.

Dale has told her where to come and what time to be there. She has it all worked out. Dale has worked part of it out for her.

She looks absolutely beautiful in red.

"I don't want to lose you," she says to Dale.

"Did you lock the door?"

She nods her head.

"I refuse to give you up!"

"Cora, go check the door. See if it's locked."

Meanwhile Dale himself looks around. Checks the windows of the empty house. He wants to be sure. From the window he looks up at the sky. It is clear. He'd been watching Cora as she came up the walkway a moment ago. Watched her climb the steps. Listening to her sounds: as she opened the unlocked door, as she entered, and as she closed the door behind herself. He felt the swelling of his cock.

Cora returns.

Cora is eating cheese and eggs. A huge pot of Canadian pea soup is cooking. Full of eggs and cheese, Cora takes a swim in a television commercial full of salad dressing. It's delicious, creamy, thick and sensuous. Canada is stuffing himself with beef and stacks of lasagne. Tons of macaroni with peas and tomatoes are baking in the oven. Cora has fled Soul Food. No more pigtails, neckbones, chitterlings, no more greens and cornbread.

2
Body Heat

I wait for that part of myself that knows more than I know. I know the words Cora, Canada, Dale.

Cora is walking along Eighth Street. A sunny spring day. She's window shopping. She bumps into an old blind woman. The woman apologizes. Cora apologizes. The word apologize has a funny shape and sound.

I wait for Cora to come back. The word Cora is here but Cora herself isn't. She's still walking along Eighth.

I smell my own body. It is an animal. I'm lying in bed. My hands have turned to claws. No. They were always claws. I have sharp dog teeth. The word dog does not conjure up a dog. These claws are not those of a tiger. I dislike cats. No. I don't dislike cats. I get up to go to the zoo. Here at the zoo I'm smelling cats. I return home to bed. Home? I'm not at home. I have no home. I'm at Cora's, waiting for her to . . . to do what? I can't trust my memory. I smell under my arms and arrange the cover over my naked body. I suddenly realize I went all the way to the Bronx Zoo naked. Nobody noticed. Body is a word nobody notices. The word naked is naked. I cover it with the word cover. I'm still waiting.

Cora is dreaming about me. I'm in a mosque in Harlem. I'm rich and militant. I have a national name. People respect me. Cora comes to see me. She confuses me with Canada. Starts talking to me about my background. Wants to know what I think of hand guns. "Hand guns should be stopped." Her eyebrows lift. She wants to know why. I tell her, "My religion begins in my body." We walk outside onto the sidewalk. Cora is still asleep.

I woke Cora in the middle of her dream. She was in the house, the one with the Gallic accent. She'd spent a lot of time in it, eating, fucking, dreaming and, of course, loving Canada, Dale, me. Waking her like that naturally had all ill effect.

"I was just admiring the rafters above my great fireplace!"

"In a wide living room?"

"Yes. And good prints in frames on the walls." Cora sighs, turns her back to my face. "And you were in it too. With your stupid pistol hidden in the kitchen in a drawer."

"It's not *my* pistol."

"It isn't *Canada's*. He was nowhere in sight."

"What'd I do with it?"

"I woke up."

"I mean. Could you *see* me with the pistol?"

"Yes. At one point you were pointing it at my head. But you were laughing."

"Then I was just playing, huh."

"You turned into Dale and I was at the kitchen sink naked except for an apron around my you know what."

"I imagined you'd be wearing something truly elegant. A cardigan evening gown or something."

"I burned my hand."

"Did I shoot?"

"You put the gun away and left the room."

"Where did I go?"

"I don't know but when you came back Canada was with you. But I couldn't tell you two apart."

"I had no character?"

"Canada had none either."

"Dale?"

"He was *in* you all this time," Cora said. "I mean: you two had become *one.*"

"Some dream."

"I woke up trying to take down the rafters. Silly, I know. Also I was planning to pull down the worn-out wheel, the chandelier."

"Wow!"

There is one thing that bugs Cora: the theory that she *can* be a mother. She has no real proof. She dreams of nursery schools. She was in one the other day. There was this unwanted child. And there was something she couldn't quite figure. Had to do with the child being handicapped. She saw herself pregnant and, for what it is worth, she also saw herself *dead.* But despite the fact Cora was dead, the child she loved, the unwanted one, was a toddler with a toy. And there was Cora trying to understand the stages of play. Child's play. Because somewhere deep in her she truly wants to be a mother—someday.

As though it's an alternative to motherhood Cora spends a lot of time before her mirror examining her skin. Her hair. The fat areas of her face. She closely inspects her mouth, its shape. Its color. She looks carefully at the lines in her hands. The back of her hands. In the mirror and otherwise. She lifts her lips back from her teeth and turns her head from side to side, looking for defects or perfections in her teeth.

Naked. Before her mirror she turns slowly. She examines her muscles. Her joints. She tries to imagine her bones beneath her flesh. She holds out her legs and turns them first this way then the other. She sees herself as a simple dry skeleton. Walking talking bones. It's funny for a minute.

Her brain. She thinks of her brain and she sees a hog's brain, the bloody veins. And it's amazing that someday her own brain will be dead, nothing but jelly—no thoughts generating from it. A permanent shock.

Cora thinks that when she sees herself in fragments she's wrong. It destroys the beauty, the entity, of her being. She hates herself for it. She has no right to do this mean thing to herself. Though life begins and ends with her body and there's nothing else except theory. Yet she has a right to her own theories but not to the destruction of her operation as a *whole* being.

In her imagination she can feel and taste the male organ. She can feel it enter her and feel its sperm, and know the release of her own egg, and hear the sounds of her own life. With her eyes she can see the blood of her cycle. And she can sweat and copulate and, hopefully, give birth. But can she?

If Cora lies in bed then stands up, she sees the print her body leaves. This is true evidence of her own existence. Nobody has to tell her, "Cora, you here."

At times she suspects she's still growing. Like a child. She has this childlike quality. You know she has it.

Plus she's left-handed.

And another good thing: her eyes are in perfect coordination with her hands. Particularly the left hand. Her eyes respect it and do as it does—usually.

She smells well too. She can smell anything worth smelling. If she isn't on downs or high. But there are odors she lives with so closely she cannot intellectually deal with them, such as: the aroma of menstruation. Or the natural juices oozing from her vagina. They're so much a part of her *being*. She operates from the inside of such odors. But Cora never thinks of her own body as an instrument possessing what we have clinically termed a "female sex organ." She knows she is the opposite of what we have, again, clinically chosen to call "male." Yet, at the same time, she knows there is *no* opposite, really. She senses each man is partly female. And each woman is, by the same token, partly male.

I try to know these things. It's harder for me though. I'm arrogant. I'm male. I have certain weaknesses springing from my orientation. I know them. I try to deal with them. I may not be very good at giving up what I imagine to be my status. I even know I imagine it and that it is not real. I know, at the same time, that Cora, operating from the core of her nature, would not choose to *re*orient her own *self* and position in the world. I mean, as *fe*-male as opposed to male.

I cook dinner. I wash dishes. I make the bed. I cook stuff like beets and carrots, baked dishes with eggplant, mushrooms, veal, chicken, fish and onions. I have spent days in Cora's kitchen making fancy casseroles. We spend hours eating and drinking. We gain weight and watch television and eat huge servings of ice cream. I bake fruit and make pies. With a sharp knife, I slice thick rough pineapples and serve them to Cora in bed. I get in bed with her and together we eat peanuts for hours. Cora and I have even fucked in a large baking pan filled with butterscotch pie. We love it!

Cora inspects the word of her mouth. She touches the paper on which her name appears. The word Cora, she thinks, is the extent of her presence. This is a word. She is sitting at the kitchen table, elbows on table. The table has a word that is used by people, like Cora, who wish to refer to it. That word is table. Cora writes her name on the paper. She erases it. It goes away but it is still there. Cora is trapped in herself. Trapped in her own imagination. When she sleeps the word sleep sleeps with her. When she dances she dances through the loops of the word dance. She draws a stick figure dancing. Canada enters the room. Dale enters the room. I enter. The three of us look at the sheet on the table. It's blank. Cora is not here.

Cora is in the bathroom inspecting the word mouth. She looks into her mouth in the mirror. The word mirror provides her with this opportunity.

I am standing behind Cora. She is wearing a thin black nightgown. The backs of her legs are lovely. I love her. The word standing allows me to watch like this. The word nightgown is what she is wearing. The nightgown itself is in her drawer with her panties. The word Cora is wearing the word nightgown. I watch the sentence: The backs of her legs are lovely.

I lie a lot. Lies are made up things. Canada lies too. He does not believe in keeping a list of things. He hates that sort of carefulness. Any attempt at order leaves him in shambles. Like that time with the demolition—list?—weapons. The FBI and the CIA investigated him. And though he is obscure now, he is still far from clear of their interest. interest.

Canada is holding the phone. "This is an obscene call. I want to come over and fuck your old lady. How about it? Let me come and fuck her in the ass. You can even watch. What about it?"

Frank Sinatra is on the screen. Eleanor Parker too. Carolyn Jones is on the screen. Canada is watching TV again. Cora is asleep in his arms.

The director asks Cora to sing *Stormy Weather*. Her attempt is brave. He asks her to tap dance. She does a few steps. The director says, "Next!"

We go to a West Indian restaurant in the Bronx. Cora orders rutabagas, fried bananas, baked sage and onions, and a lentil salad; this is just the beginning. The main dish consists of ham, beef, chicken, pork, mushrooms, creole fried eggs and potatoes, topped with a thick creamy cheese sauce.

I have only a hamburger.

After Cora's desert of ice cream, cheese cake, apple pie and fruit cake, I—with the help of a waiter—have to carry her home on a stretcher.

The next morning she's fine. She knocks off a dozen eggs.

Cora is walking slowly to the laundry. Her pace is slow. She carries a heavy bag on her back. She's trying to remember every man who's ever made love with her. She can't. She thinks of five men, their cocks hard and their eyes hard, but those five only fucked her hard and now, she cannot remember their names. Some of the men in her past were snobs. Others chatterboxes in bed. None of them were aware of being words themselves suspended in space on a page. At least six were in show business. Two loved to do ballet steps. One, like Cora, was born in Atlanta. Twelve were two-time losers.

Cora still walks slowly to the laundry. At an

intersection a drunk white man driving a huge blue truck shouts, *"Hello pussy!"*

Cora smiles brightly and gives him the finger.

The laundry is called Hades. The grocery store next door is also called Hades. The shoe repair shop too.

Once the clothes are washing in the machine, Cora sits on the bench, looking out the window at the moving traffic. A truck called Hades goes by. A boy carrying the head of a goat runs along the sidewalk. Two cops walk, holding hands.

There's no point in talking, yet we go on talking. Cricket frogs jump about on the tables. Whistling tree frogs are in our bedrooms. Patch-nosed snakes crawl under the beds. Spotted turtles and map turtles sit for hours on the kitchen floors. Blind snakes are in the dirty clothes containers. Every movie we see on television has been produced by Darryl F. Zanuck. Here, we're fucking around with ideas.

"Cora, stop fucking around."
But she couldn't stop laughing.
"Cut it out, now."

A few days later. "I think Canada has been lying, stealing and cheating."
"But Cora."
"The motherfucker."
"Maybe he was an over-dependent child."
"He's a motherfucker."
"Maybe, Cora, he was a lazy child."

"A motherfucker."

"Urban or rural?" I said.

"Motherfucker. Where is he anyway?"

"I'm right here, bitch! Do you want to repeat those remarks you just made!"

Cora quickly left. The door slammed behind her. She went away with that admirable gait of strong female self-confidence. And Canada's anger cooled.

Two girls are coming up the street side by side. Both look like Cora. But neither is. Both are wearing soft colors of blue and the raindrops splash off their clothing in an interesting way. I don't know why it is interesting.

Canada and I are sitting in a restaurant having coffee, and quietly looking through the large window at the street, the traffic, the people. Two girls, both in red, go by. One looks like Cora. But she isn't. It is the way she walks. A sexy stride.

Canada stands and goes across the room to the coin-operated telephone on the wall. He inserts a dime and dials a number. He speaks into the mouthpiece. He says, "Tales and myths about genes and chromosomes." So naturally I wonder who he's talking to. Who would be interested in such chatter. He continues to speak but I miss most of what he says. Yet some of it comes across the room to me. "You take karate and yoga. Vitamins. Take your body temperature. Who are your ancestors. All these things. Hunger and thirst. Ergonomics. Your mind and your environment."

Finally, Canada returns. "Who?"

"Cora."

"Canada," I said, "what's going on."

"Genes and chromosomes. Your environment."

I laugh. "Come on, now."

"Seriously. Relaxation. Keeping fit."

I take a sip of the coffee.

"Growth," he says.

"Your face lies."

"Growth, physique and racial differences."

"Canada, fuck off." My laughter is uneasy.

"Why are you depressed?"

"I don't know." I thought about it. "Crank calls, I guess. Nightmare voices screaming in my ears. The blues."

"You're tripping."

The phone is ringing again. Dale answers. It's Canada, he says, "The number you have reached is disconnected. This is a recording. The number you have reached is not mine. This is not the number you want."

Cora goes to the toilet. She has a book with her. She sits there crapping and reading: "Cora is putting on a dress. It's blue with white flowers. Her lips are pressed tightly together."

The cops working on the case recently returned from the moon. They have Human Achievements papers. The lunar conquest aroma is still heavy where they go. People throw star dust at them.

They follow me everywhere. Every time I drive faster than sixty miles per hour they stop me. Want to see everything I got. They finger their pistols, ready to shoot me.

Cops are over my head right now in hydrogen balloons. They aint doing nothing constructive but they mean well.

The police manage themselves and often they get their work done. They move around each other. I see their fat blue uniforms. Wool or cotton, it doesn't much matter. At this distance. The white metal of their badges. Some metalsmith somewhere has pride in what he does. These policemen seem strange moving about. Some of them cannot bend at the knee. A stiffness. The one with the flat device for taking fingerprints moves only about as much as a tree trunk. A face the color of a limestone region. He's the one involved in the initial work on Cora's death. Two other cops told him not to use the device but it was his first chance and, well, action comes before words. Yet he had a difficult time trying to do it without bending his knees.

"Rigor mortis hasn't set in," one cop said.

"It is like the roof of a cave."

"Yes, but nothing has collapsed," another one said.

"I feel a flow of cold air."

"You always do."

"Yes, but nothing has a roof—not around here."

"Did you get her name yet?"

"I have the instant negatives. I put the silicone beneath her skin for the prints. I looked in all the corners and in the closets."

"What about the body of the man?"

"Same. We're checking him out."

"He looks cooled by radiation."

"You'd look that way too."

They each continued to move slowly around each other. Some stopped moving and started talking. From time to time, others continued to move cautiously.

"We've been here before."

"Yes, but it is the difference between a long story and a short one. In a long one you simply return to the scene of the crime. Often. Over and over until you get your percentage of words. Then you go home."

The one with the Polaroid MP-3 camera went to the window and looked out. "Phew! What a fucking dreary view!"

Two others walked over and stood behind him, looking over his shoulders. Meanwhile one peeling rubber gloves from his sweaty hands: "I don't see nothing!"

"Here," the one with the camera said, "hold this camera." And one of the men behind him took it. This left the cameraman's hands free.

He took from his vest pocket a toothpick and began picking his teeth. "Such a fucking dreary mess."

They had taken the bodies out and away.

The one with the scapel who's scraped up blood, now stood behind the cop with the hacksaw, watching him work on the edge of the window.

"Be careful."

"Don't worry, boss," the hacksaw man said, "I have a feeling for this sort of thing. And I trust myself."

"As long as you know."

Canada and I go to a bar for drinks. There's a television set over the bar. Along the bar, men and women with beer bellies are watching the screen. The Jefferson Airplane is bringing in more cops to investigate the deaths of Cora and Dale. The anchor man says: "You may have to wait for that part of yourself that knows more than you know, to figure this one out. There are no trustworthy clues. A promising young Black Greenwich Village stage actress, Cora

TO: _____

MESSAGE:

Cloth edition is
OSI.
We are sending
paper.

Write or Phone us for Additional Information.

Academic Book Center, Inc.

5345 N.E. SANDY BLVD.
PORTLAND, OREGON 97213
(503) 288-3152

Hull, and an unidentified man may have taken their own lives lives today. . ."

Cora is playing the piano. Playing Mozart. Can't remember what. A mule deer stands in the center of the floor. The olympic games are on television. *Gone With the Wind* has just been published. I'm beside myself with agony. The Lindberghs are out. Snow is falling. It's summer!

Cricket frogs are jumping all over the street. This is a novel of manners. Characters spend hours trying to decide what they want to do. Grant Wood is a painter who turns up just this one time.

The three of us were sitting together at a table in a Greenwich Village restaurant. Canada didn't like the area but he tolerated it. He felt more at home in Harlem. Cora, on the other hand, loved the Village.

"Is it your stomach?" I asked her.

"All over. Sick."

"Pregnant?"

"No. Yes. No, not possible!"

"Would you mind it?"

"I'd be it, that way."

"Maybe," said Canada, sipping something through a straw at the left side of his mouth. "Maybe, Cora, you've always been pregnant. Maybe all women are, from their beginning to forever, pregnant."

I said to Canada, "How about me?"

"Men?" He chuckled. "You're the *inside*, the other side, the outside. You should stay where you are. Nameless."

"I have no shape. I *am* nameless. I don't try to defend myself, but Cora deserves a word."

"She has her name."

"Something is always wrong with a code, a symbol."

"It makes you," said Cora.

"You're sick."

"I feel weak, but better."

I got up and went across the room to the jukebox. I pushed a number labeled "Digestive System." A rock group called Bone took off on it, blasting.

When I got back to the table the first phrase I caught was "test-tube babies," from Cora.

"But what about carbon-copy children?"

"Check yourself, Canada. There aren't any."

I sat down politely, quiet.

"But why are we sitting here?" I said. "We've finished eating the survival food."

"I'm finishing my cigarette," Cora said. But she wasn't smoking.

A beautifully dressed queen came into the place throwing ass left-right in great rhythm.

"Look," Canada said.

"I see."

"Don't look," Cora said. "He's as revolutionary as anybody revolutionary. He breaks things and ideas. I like him."

"You like every freak," Canada said.

"That's why I like you, fuckface."

The loud record came to an end.

Cora cleared her throat. "We're building something here in this relationship, the three of us."

"Things are slipping away."

"Canada, you're not sensitive enough," she said.

"But he knows," I said.

"He is."

"I am."

"You are."

Canada gets high and listens to jazz—or call it Black music. A stack of Armstrong Ella Prez Bird Billie on the turntable sets him straight for hours.

Cora enters, very annoyed. She was in Baltimore doing a show. No. She didn't get the part. Still she was there and everything went well. The show was called *Hey Baba Rebop* and Cora had the lead. She sang and danced beautifully. She was made a big star overnight. She returned to New York with Broadway in the palm of her hand. Singing, *Honeysuckle Rose*!

Murder scares shit out of me. I would rather deal with the problems of taste buds. I would rather count the cells in sperm than to deal with murder. I would rather paste the word Atlanta onto the city of Atlanta. They say people who kill themselves as an act of murder are not on good terms with the word murder. Murder is an incident. It happens. Words, especially words like murder and incidents, hide under beds and in closets, they are so guilty.

The boy in a green shirt pretends his name is Hades and that he understands murder. He tells no one. He dreams, daydreams of going on the stage and getting a leading role alongside Cora in *Guys and Dolls*.

Murder is sent to Cora through the mail. No, it is not a magazine. It comes as something jumping around in a brown paperbag.

Cora does not pretend to know murder. Even Canada does not know murder. He is a man who spends time making up things. Writing words on paper has a powerful effect on his mind. If he writes murder, it means something terrible has happened. He waits for reactions.

I wait for reactions.

We're all kids again, growing up in the same neighbor-hood. Spinning the bottle.

I get Cora. We go behind the gym. I fuck her in the grass. She gets pregnant. I marry her. We have ten children. I work at the steel mill. I'm in the union. Cora hates me. My children hate me. I want to die, they want to die. I'm tense. Uneasy.

I brag about how much money I make. I'm very tense.

I'm ashamed of myself.

Properly the tension should build. Yet the situation is worse. It doesn't matter whether it is proper or not. I cannot know all of it anyway. I see I am close enough to Cora to speak to her. She stands a little to the left of Canada who is hiding something behind his back. His hands are behind his body. If my guess is correct he is holding a large glossy snap-shot of Cora hugging Dale. The picture shows the right side of Dale's face and the upper portion of his body, and what you can see of Cora, is mainly her left tit, her left hip, her left arm and the left side of her face. Her eyes are closed. Dale's aren't. Yet I may be dead wrong about all of this.

In fact the tension *does* build. They keep coming around each other. Even Dale comes around a lot now. He may be the one we like the least, still we must see him as he comes around. And hear him speak. Everybody talks some-times. And everybody listens, sometimes.

Too often they want to know *why*. But I, being the way I am, am at peace with being. Sometimes. I hate them when they want me to be clear. Cora asked me if I had a point of view. A message. Canada, a few years ago, wanted to know why I repressed my anger, how I let it out. Since obviously it has to come out some way. It comes out all right. Dale seems to laugh his away. It's all right. I know

you've never heard him laugh. I don't feel responsible to him.
I am not supposed to show you how he laughs. Mostly he did
his laughing in private anyway. With Cora close. Their bodies
often dripping with each other's sweat.

I always think I'm not going to be able to pull them
away from each other. Canada too. I mean when Canada and
Cora are together. Not just in bed. At tables. Or on streets,
simply walking. I keep hoping though. I can't go on like this,
the doubt. And yet when they work well together there is no
reason to pull them apart. A few days ago the small talk was
dreary, too much. I felt bad and had to go home, to bed.
Sleep the depression away.

Then I come back to them. Sometimes they don't
want to do anything but move around each other. No drama
except the simple drama of existence. I shouldn't complain.
Very often it is better when they choose not to speak to each
other. When I take over and talk like I'm talking now. At
least, in this way, I work off my own tension. Which, you
know, is where they get theirs.

Get to this: Cora isn't based on anybody.

Dale isn't anything.

Canada is just something I'm busy making up.

I am only an act of my own imagination. I cannot
even hear my own voice the way they hear it. I got the
"Bullfrog Blues."

Cora does the "Charleston Rag."

Dale sings "Hello Dolly."

Canada covers the waterfront.

John Wayne rang the doorbell. Cora opened the door.
"Howdy ma'am, I'm looking for a little biddy ol' prairie dog
that might have wandered this way. He wouldn't mean much
to anybody but me."

"Wait." Cora returned with a snapshot of Canada.
"Like this?"

"Nope. That aint him. Guess I have to try next door."

Cora rushes along her street, returning from a rehearsal. A dark boy in a green shirt is leading a blind man along. The boy looks at Cora. "This is Spencer Tracy. I'm taking him home for dinner. Mama fix fried bananas!"

Cora sometimes goes to the basement to wash her clothes. She's there now. The boy is in the dryer screwing a dream he's kept in his pocket for weeks. Cora takes it from him and gives him a kiss. He blushes and hides under the washing machine.

Running, I lose my shoe. The post office is still sending my mail to the old address. I'm wearing only an undershirt. A young white woman stops me. I must know her. Says she's Cora's friend. I must hurry because I'm half naked. She understands. Offers me a dollar to buy a pair pants. As I leave, thanking her, she says, "Take care, Canada."

In a nearby Salvation Army Store I search for blue jeans.

Cora says she woke up speaking. Saying, "Swollen breakfast," which makes no sense at all. And as her head cleared, she heard a knocking at what apparently was the front door. She went to the door, naked on tiptoe, and peeped through the keyhole. Standing there, a white man in suit and tie looked impatient. His eyes were focused on the peephole. Well certainly there was no point in opening the door for a character like this. Probably a bill collector and Cora had no money—no extra money. Especially not for bill collectors.

She tells me these things, these incidents, and I listen closely. Sometimes I am a good listener. But I often only pretend to hear. So far I've met no one who's better at pretending. I have this vision of myself putting someone on. The person focuses, it is Cora. Only I can't deceive her for long. She's too good in her knowledge of me. I made her and like a child who *senses* its mother, Cora senses me. With such knowledge my elusive stance becomes difficult, if not funny. I wish everything were funny all the time and I could spend the rest of my life laughing. I don't want to think. When I have to deal with Cora I'm forced to think too much. I'd rather drink beer with Cora and not try to untangle the mystery of her presence and her dreams of swollen food. Couldn't be anything but sex.

The time I was sick in bed she brought medicine. Hung around telling me her dreams. And I was trying selfishly to understand my own symptoms. The day before I fell ill I'd been wandering around in a dusty bookstore run by a dried up little old man; wondered about his life away from the store; wondered if his body had a difficult fight against the possibility of disease. How often did he go to the doctor for a checkup. But how about me, and pills and my aging body. Saw a man with one leg wobbling along on an artificial limb. *What is my skin?* How do I live in it?

Cora came to play nurse that time. Despite her disorders and her artificial dreams, her diet and her pills. I talked with her about herself. Told her she was a transplanted bitch. I felt evil—*alive*—that day! But quietly she continued to look after me without trying to challenge me. She knew I was out of my mind.

I know I'm *in* my mind. What I really want, though, is to be *out* of it. I would like nothing better, at the moment, than to wander around outside myself. See what the world *is* from another angle.

Hello. For the moment I am somebody else. I'm John Milton. I'm Boris Karloff. I'm Zola. In England, in Hollywood, in France, the world slips through my fingers. I run around like crazy, trying to find the Cross Bronx Expressway. If I can find it, I'll know how to get back.

I'm running alongside the traffic. Headed south. People driving by in their cars look curiously into my eyes.

Schizy schizy schizy! Happy one minute, sad the next, Cora and I are spending the summer together. We picnic in Jenny Jump Forest, New Jersey, and in front of the Minisink Monument in Minisink Ford, New York, at Pocono Knob. While in the Poconos, we eat a ton of apples in Apple Valley Village, and tour Memorytown USA, and make love under the waterfall at Buck Hill.

You're on a train moving along the countryside in a foreign land. Two men in your compartment are talking about pipes and drills. A fat lady sleeps with a frog on her lap. Who are you? You're the author. You're writing a letter to Dale: "If you are only a word then Cora was alone when she died. If explosion and death are only words then nothing happened." You will mail the letter at the next stop. You don't know it, but you're in Canada, headed for Cora.

The policemen who were sent to talk to us intro-duced themselves as "the finest from the department," and ended their introduction with the curious statement: "Canada Jackson, you're not really under suspicion. We suspect you *know* something though."

"I know my name."

"One thing we don't quite trust is your name."

Canada cleared his throat. "You guys may not know it but everybody in the community suspects you planted the bomb to make it look like a Black militant plot so you'd have what appears to be a chance of going up side any Black person's head."

"Nonsense."

They were both white and fat and forty or so. They were standing in the middle of Canada's living room.

I watched from inside Canada's head. He wasn't mad at me anymore. Apparently having accepted my advantage over him, he saves his energy for situations and ideas he can handle and leaves me alone. But I'm never alone. It is either Canada or Cora and sometimes Dale.

"I shouldn't have let you guys in. There were cops here this morning asking the same questions you're asking, saying the same shit. I'm under suspicion, I'm not under suspicion. What fucking difference does it make!"

"They're playing games with you Canada," I whis-pered. I whispered because I didn't want the fatheads to hear. And I was only half sure I wanted Canada himself to hear. But the words were out and he heard me loud and clear. "Put 'em out."

His heart began to beat faster. I felt the growing uneasiness. I couldn't make up my mind what to do. Just sit tight, things will change.

Canada finally said, "Look, you guys will have to split. I got things to do."

"Sure," one said. "We move through the years."

"Well. Move through the impact. Leave by way of the door. There is a grand future out there beyond."

"Help them, Canada. Look at the door yourself. See it."

"I try but I see one where the paint peals."

"It's good enough to leave by."

"But it's not designed for them."

"They have blood on their hands and they sniff the sick and injured, rob the pockets of the dead and fuck puppies." I was getting very angry.

Canada laughed softly. But, in what felt like one motion, he moved to the door and snatched it open and held it that way. Waiting for the meatheads to leave.

After the cops left I closed my aching eyes and tried to see Cora's mouth. I felt her presence. But I was a little worried about my own interpretation. I could, of course, deal with the things I saw and felt: but lately I was having a lot of trouble handling the *ideas* of things and situations. And dreams.

If I was beginning to dream of Cora apparently I chose not to remember the enormous cave of those trips into her, around and around in her. Canada called sometimes in the wee hours of the morning. He couldn't sleep. He seemed frantic. He'd ramble on about Cora. He'd cry.

I'd sleep and dream of her mound and of vacant spaces in strange crowded areas, unclear in my mind. I'd struggle through a sulphur yellow light, my hands stretched before me. I'd feel the sponginess of Cora's tongue inside my own mouth. But I'd always wake up.

I wasn't sleeping well in those days. I sleep very poorly now. I feel a strange wave frequency—has something to do with Cora. The kind of vibes she gives off.

I wake up and turn away. I go out and walk and turn corners and have terrible visions and check myself. Stop.

I think I will make it to the end without losing my balance. I will take the word balance with me. Till now I had reasonable doubt.

There is a large living creature under Cora's bed. It looks like Canada. I'm on my hands and knees, looking under the bed. It is not Canada. It looks like Cora.

I am under Cora's bed. The word bed hides me. I cannot go on pretending I am safe from . . .

I keep hoping for smoothness.

"I look out toward the objects of the afternoon," says Canada. His voice is recorded and comes from the radio. I am in Cora's place, listening. When he finishes, a program called Hades comes on. It is full of people concerned with thresholds living out their lives in New England.

I go to the kitchen for a glass of spring water. All around me are fingerprints, fingerprints all over everything . . .

I remember too much. I half remember things. I don't know the incidents which I should keep in mind. Cora, your protagonist, even when she is no longer here, occupies too much of my strength. The time and energy I give to Cora I might give to myself. Trying to come out of this—and be more direct, to make a clear and easy passage. You may want to walk close to my edge. For all I know Cora may come back. She may return with relative success and she may bring at least a veneer of comfort—for herself, if not for anyone else. And if she succeeds in attaining a vestige of peace, then I too may have a chance. I want my chance but right now my chances look mean and stingy. I try hard not to remember the particular things that might wreck them. Small as they are.

I try to come closer to her but it hurts too much. The closer I get the deeper the pain. My hands ache.

She's stretched out on a stack of pillows. Her eyes are closed. Her mouth is open. The muscles in my hands ache intensely.

I close my eyes and fall on my knees beside the bed. Tears pouring, I try to open my eyes and stop. But I can't stop or stand up. I am shaking all over. The tension builds. I'm losing my balance.

You're ice skating in Canada. Your name is Cora. Your story is based on known variables. You want to be a successful actress but your agent—your agent?—yes, your agent, the author, tells you you are only an extrapolation. Your toilet training and intellectual experience are not in order. You need to clean up your act.

You're figure skating near the border. You're arrested for being too fragmented.

At one point they thought they had definitely established to whom the suitcase belonged. Close investigation revealed their mistake. As it stands, nobody knows. The little boy in the washed out green shirt said he knew. But he lies. I see him now: dark hands and a dark face. He moves in the dim hallway, sad. He misses Cora.

"Hi."

He blushes.

I have no intention of making him feel uneasy. The boy obviously already feels uneasy: born that way. How else. Under muddy yellow light. What sort of equilibrium can he be expected to maintain. He responded to Cora's affection. He now seems absolutely friendless. Canada drove him out.

"Hello," I say again.

He says nothing. The hallway smells stronger than ever of fresh and stale piss. It is a crucial place. Under the stairway, Cora has told me, kids fuck quickies, drop their rubbers and run. Junkies shoot up too. Wineheads sleep.

Finally he hides in the shadow of the doorway to his apartment. Suddenly the door is opened by a fat woman.

"Come in here! What for you hang out here like this, huh?" She is screeching at him.

Warm waves slap behind my eyelids. My brain is buzzing. I feel an inner shiver. I climb the steps slowly. Canada probably won't be home. A wasted trip, wasted energy, wasted space.

But the peephole opens and an eye winks. After I've knocked three times. I know I'm crazy but I hope—against all hope—it is Cora. Please person be Cora. Just this once be Cora. You are Cora person. Please.

I believe it is guilt that drives me to Canada. Guilt now because there isn't and there never was a true friendship between us. There was no trust way back when. And now. Well now things are clearly worse. Despite the fact we seem to be together always in some way, we never quite touch or really speak to or hear each other. And I have never smelled him.

"Have a seat, old pal."

The chair is at an angle from the mirror. And I see myself reflected there. Behind me is Cora holding her breasts, one in each hand, examining the nipples. I shiver. I want to touch her and feel something.

Canada leaves the room and returns with the pistol. He takes a seat on the edge of the bed. Unloads it and reloads it. "She was everything," he said, "and she was nothing. Her mind too worked that way."

"What's the gun for."

"Those wet things crawling up her legs."

"Canada. Are you . . . "

"The window. I closed it. She opens it. I . . . "

"You . . . what?"

"Her tongue, her hairline. I liked the shape of her head. The way she walked. Her talk. She was trying, 'to overthrow the desperation, the tension of each second'."

"And," I said, "to find her own style."

"No. Her meaning. She left the kitchen door open. The sun would shine into the kitchen and sometimes she'd play the radio all day. I shouldn't have spoiled things."

"You did your best."

"I spoiled her and I gave her nothing. Not even myself. I put her through hell. And she was simply trying to learn to handle her demons."

"In another time *they* would have killed her anyway."

"Why? Because she winked at little boys or because she picked her nose."

"You're an echo, Canada. Look in the mirror."

"From here I can't see. I see only you."

"So you see me."

"I'm going to put the pistol back with the silverware. Excuse me."

He returned with his hands in his pockets. Somebody under the bed coughed. We looked at each other. Canada stood close to the mirror, looking at the image of his own face. Image is the word. Then, like a century of painful people, he broke into expensive sobbing. A funny light danced through the room. The sound of fingersnapping filled the place and things started moving around on their own. However, when Canada finished and was laughing, everything was all right. He turned on the television and the word seemed normal as all get out.

Remembering she was supposed to be smart, Cora went to the library to try to find a book to read. She went through the titles. *Love in Hades* by Painy F. Sobben, *Pistol in the Dream* by Landstep Printcardy; on and on, like that; so she gave up. The only book that sort of halfway aroused her interest was something called *Model Criminal Investigation.* Even this she passed up. The cover was dull.

She ran home, went to sleep and dreamed she was in the Kingdom of Navarre being raped by thousands of Spanish and French soldiers. It was no fun being sore and all, so she woke and ate a whole cream cheese pie and a gallon of pure ice cream.

I'm parachuting from an F8U jet fighter at forty-seven thousand feet in a thunderstorm. Temperature seventy degrees. The Van Wyck Expressway is below. I'm aiming for the Whitestone Bridge but I'm way off. On the way down I'm trying to decide what to do next. I could go to Indonesia and ride a sumba pony. Climb a mountain or marry Cora. By the way the F8U is called *Cora.* A fighter, I was trained near the Canadian border.

I land on the Belt Parkway. My three characters are waiting for me.

I tend to see very little of the surface. Cora's face for example. Another example. My own face. With Cora one should be more literal. After all she is very physical. She *was* a very physical person. Cora was the opposite of me. She took people and things at face value. She took people at their word. I hardly know how to take people. I spend too much time sunk deep in my own wanderings far down below the surface, dreaming up problems for myself. Where I don't have them I invent them, and at least I tell myself it is what sustains me. What wakes me up. The challenge each day. Canada is a problem. I mean I have to deal with all kinds of things. People and situations. How will Canada adjust to Cora's death. Who cares about Dale's absence. If no one, why no one. Who was he, where'd he come from. What did Cora see in him. Vice versa.

And my being alone so much reinforces the tendency to skin-dive beneath the surface. Not that I find solutions. I should ideally strike a balance between the surface and the lower depths. I can do the low stuff very effectively. I need practice on the surface where Cora, Canada and Dale hang out.

I lie here like this, thinking. I stay in bed too much. It makes me afraid of myself. But then apathy is good sometimes. It helps one through the rough spots. The windows rattle. The season is changing. I change. Cora is dead. Canada is drunk. Dale is dead. My eyes are open but I see nothing. That's not true. I do see: I see blue darkness. I haven't yet decided what to do about myself. I don't know how I feel about Cora's death. I refuse to think that I'll never see her again. Never is too terrible to understand. *Cora Hull.* "Cora Hull," I say. Dark space. No answer. I say, "Cora." And know there will never be an answer. Since there never was.

The windows rattle because the season is changing. Leaves have dropped from trees and people are wrapping themselves beneath huge coats. We begin with the body and end with the body. Anything else is a theory. Soon I doubt if I'll be able to still visualize her face.

Cora is looking through the stained glass window of a mosque. Inside, Canada is crossing the arctic region, he has huskies pulling him on a sled. She calls him but he can't hear. I take Cora's hand and lead her down the street to a cathedral. Together, we stand in the huge doorway, looking in. We see Dale, dressed as a cowboy, on an Anglo-Arab horse. His saddle is English. His feet are not in the stirrups. The landscape around him is obviously Sioux Falls, South Dakota.

I take Cora to the zoos. At Beardsley Park and Zoo in Bridgeport, we freak out on the elegant birds; in our rented Nash, we stop at Old MacDonald's Farm, South Norwalk, and watch kiddies feeding huge snakes to tiny ducks on a pond. Then to Turtle Back Zoo in West Orange. Up to Bear Mountain for a screw in the bushes. And back to New York City for the real zoo.

I want to stop dwelling on her and get myself together. She believed in me, I think. She believed in herself too. Which was probably why she was able to believe in me. But I don't know why she did. I never did anything profound to deserve her trust. I just promised myself to stop thinking about her. But she possessed such an amazing capacity to show affection—even through her dreamy and often even dreary cynicism. Yet I can't knock her too much. It destroys me.

Cora went through a women's liberation phase. Every time I opened my mouth something wrong came out. For awhile she had me feeling very uptight. This connection

between words and feelings. I did not want to be unhappy.
Yet I wanted most of all to hold my convictions, whatever
they were. I can't remember. I was changing. Not necessarily
growing but simply changing. At least for one week during
that terrible and beautiful month, she was reading a lot of
underground women's newspapers and magazines and ranting
and raving and lecturing me. And I learned something. I
listened to her. My aggression was not always all physical or
mental. But when she reached the theory of some revolutionary woman who said they (all women) must disavow
relationships with men in order to get the revolution started,
Cora stopped. Said they were absolutely insane!

I'm somewhere different. The place is huge. Lit with
purple lights. People are doing the cakewalk. The joint is
jumping. The band is gutbucket and greasy with funk.
Couples are rubbing bellies and slobbering each other. The
base is a bitch.

The MC goes to the mike. "License plate
C.A.N.A.D.A., please move your car. It's too close to the
threshold."

Forgetting that my name is not really Canada, I rush
out and drive the car away. I park in on a dark deserted street
and return to the dance.

I'm driving an early American mail coach along a long
dirt road. Six Iceland ponies are straining to pull me and the
load of special deliveries. They're all from Canada. Many of
them are addressed to Cora. A few to Dale. I stop in front of
the Brooklyn Museum to ask the guard how to get to
Manhattan. He takes me on a tour of the museum, showing
me various abstract paintings. "These things are about

themselves. Look at the paint. By the way, did you put a dime in the parking meter?"

The time Canada brought his fist down on the table and shook everything off, I tried to pretend I wasn't sitting there. I didn't want to understand his anger. Nor could I safely acknowledge it. Cora turned from the kitchen sink to see what was going on. Through his dark glasses he looked at her with disgust. He'd spilled ale on his yellow ochre shirt.

"Bring me that pistol."

Cora opened the silverware drawer and brought the gun to her man. He took it. Smiled cynically.

She returned to the dishes in the sink and Canada checked the weapon, then aimed it at me. He held it like that. And I tried not to show fear.

"Light a cigarette for me."

From the pack of Viceroy on the table I took a cigarette, lit it and handed it to him, cautiously. Meanwhile I squeezed my mind off from thought.

Then from the sink, Cora said, "Canada."

But he didn't answer.

Again she said, "Canada!" And not waiting for him to reply she continued, "Come unscrew the top on this jar—please!"

From the corners of my eyes I could see her looking at us. I still refused to let my mind work. Let alone speak. I felt a word from me at that moment might have been terrible.

"Canada!" Cora shouted.

Finally he stood up and left the gun lying on the table. While he was at the sink beside Cora fumbling with the jar, I took a close look at the gun. I mean, I put on my glasses and leaned halfway across the table. It was not a gun. I was stunned. No. I was only half surprised. The object was clearly a fancy can opener. Well I felt better toward Canada. We were still friends after all? If we ever had been. He was only playing a game? After all I was not composed of metal.

I've presently reduced myself to Canada. I'm Canada. Cora and I are picnicking in a dale near Dingmans Falls in the Poconos. We have ham wine cheese nuts. We run out of wine. I fly to California for more. When I return Cora's gone. A note pinned to the picnic basket says: "If you love me come and get me. I'm at Turntable Junction in Jersey with Dale."

A huge balloon floats overhead. Cora is up there waving to me. I'm swimming in the swimming pool of a motel in Los Angeles. This morning a picture postcard came from Canada. It shows him defusing a bomb. The New York Police Department will soon give him an award.

Cora is coming down slowly.

I'm high diving.

Dale is shooting Canada from a cannon up to meet Cora.

Organisms live blankly together. But as I say I can't tell you whether or not Dale has *meaning*. You know he won't focus properly. To know anything specific about his whereabouts is even less likely. Nowadays no one has this particular sort of skill anyway. Take machines. Though they break down, they tend to be more precise. Yet the data they offer on Dale (stuff like his social security number, driver's license number, telephone number or apartment number) are, except in the smallest way, nonfunctional. Yet his penis, you know, many times was a huge problem in Cora (though perhaps not to her). I know there's something savage in myself I am repressing. Well. I have rights! I had learned to live with the idea of Canada with Cora, but Dale . . .

One day I passed them on a busy street. Walking together. Nothing between them but their hands, wet warm skin no doubt. But even on a clear day, such as that one, his face was far from sharp—actually it was more out of focus than it usually was in the dimness of some softly lit apartment. The thing that stands out in my mind is *how* his hand gripped Cora's. The way they were swinging their arms. His coat sleeve, now that much of it too, comes back. Poor Cora. Always tried for her *own*. To be herself, searching blindly. But Dale still won't let me speak for him. I don't blame him one bit. Even now I still possess Cora. In a way she can't be taken away. But I'm too possessive. Yet I try desperately not to be; realizing that I not only cannot *own* her, but also I cannot even begin to own myself. My own movements belong to someone else. These words even, are not mine. They are still strange in my head. The thoughts and feelings beneath them are not friendly.

Canada unlocked the door and entered. Leaving it standing open, a square view of the hallway—a way toward the outside. I cleared my throat and waited.

"The motherfucker's name is Dale."

"Evans?"

"No."

I've decided to try to make peace with Dale. I rent a car. It's summer and I want to take my three friends on a trip. Cora sits beside me. I'm driving. Dale and Canada are in back. We move north on 95, through White Plains, on up through Connecticut, Massachusetts and New Hampshire. In New Hampshire we visit a forest full of yellow and pink flowers. We drink tons of spring water and fall asleep in the bottom of a very dry riverbed.

When I wake I'm alone.

Cora has a part in a play. All she has to do is sit and knit. Canada, in the same play, sits on a pole. Dale has to smash a piano to smithereens. I carry the wreckage off stage before the curtain closes. The first curtain takes place back in the seventeenth century.

For real this time, I'm log rolling for a living. Canada is the boss. Cora is his wife. Dale is the strawboss. We're in the Northwest. We smoke Marboro cigarettes. We don't talk much.

Someone is trying desperately to open the door to the apartment. The wiggling key makes a hell of a noise. Meanwhile I am watching Cora dance. Cora is watching herself, step by ballet step, from the mirror. My stomach aches and my heart swells. Something spectacular is about to happen—though there is no evidence. But you know how you know, without clues. Are we really clandestine. Why do I feel guilty. I'm innocent. Cora is not guilty. Why should I think of hiding in the closet. What sort of tradition is that. So what if I fit behind garments. What deep fear is this at the root of jealousy. What is the evil in jealousy; what is its crime. Is it innocent.

The person outside continues to turn the key. Cora dances close to the mirror and, without losing rhythm, she kisses her own lips on the mirror.

"Why you never give me anything. I like gifts."

"Rejuvenation."

The noise of the key continues. I feel hungry and thirsty.

"I've got your rejuvenation. I want a gift."

"I give you relaxation."

"You give me menopause."

"I give you tissues."

"You give me your face."

"I give you balance."

"You give me tales."

"I give you muscle."

"You give me sleep."

"I give you sperm."

"The truth is, dear friend, you give me a pain in the age."

"Cora, I give you my vitamins and my growth."

"You give me Canada. He's all."

"Not true. I give you energy."

"I suppose you give me life too."

"I give you life."

"Enzymes."

"Cora, I give you gifts. I gave you a sense of history and art and literature. I gave you man in space."

"You gave me hunger and a male sex organ."

"Taste buds and nerve endings."

"Sure. And they're pointless."

Now at last the door opens. And since no one is there, I understand even less.

We're all saints in the desert buried alive up to our necks. We're praying. Canada, Dale, Cora and I have changed radically. We're asking the Christian God to forgive us for our sinful bodies. To suffer like this is to atone.

I'm alone again, on an inland waterway in a rowboat. Rowing is difficult. I'm headed for an inlet called Cora. Wild blackberry and holly trees grace the shores. A kid in a green shirt on a Dülmen pony waves from the roof of a yellow house.

Cora has an X-ray of her own brain, one of her heart, one of her vagina, I mean her womb; she also has a set of X-rays showing her bone structure. She has these things framed and they hang in the living room. Though other people do, she herself hardly notices them anymore. Even during that short time, a week, when she was overly concerned with racial differences and classification of human types. And searching her own name, *Hull*, and ancestry. But that was months ago.

"Give me your left hand."

I held my left hand toward Cora.

"Hhhhhh . . . "

"You see features?"

"I see proprioception."

"You see man under great stress, woman."

"Perhaps. But I see lifeline and I see character."

"Character? Well. How about cells?"

"I see your face in your hand. I also see sex appeal."

"I too see sex appeal."

"I see," Cora said with a smirk, "love!"

"You see race prejudice too? How about kinship?"

"I see no kinship, no conflict, no animal behavior."

"Look at your own hand."

"Give me your right hand."

"I'm not your idol. Where is Canada?"

"Let him out if you want him. You keep him locked away in your adolescence. Let him change roles. I want to change roles too. I want deliverance from marriage."

"Conformity."

"I hate institutions."

"You hate attitudes. Give me back my hand."

She released my hand and laughed.

"Problem child," she said.

"Yeah, but is this the nature of courtship?"

"It is called *patterns* of deviance."

"But I thought . . . "

"You always think."

"I fear the world of middle age. Why?"

"You love pregnant snakes and field rats. Why?"

"I need friendship," I said.

"You make me wonder sometimes."

"My attitude is religious. And you, Cora, sometimes you are as traditional as a small town housewife. You shop carefully through my skull for the best cabbage and carrots."

Naked, Cora stood before the window looking down at a sharp angle upon the heads of people moving across pavement. The tops of cold painted cars.

I sat in a corner in a chair. Waiting for the key to turn in the door. But the door is unlocked; then perhaps someone will come and lock it, lock us in forever. With each other.

I'm restless. I leave New York more and more. Cora travels with me. We're in a hick motel in Elmira. Cora's sitting on the bed playing with her toes. I'm trying to watch television but I can't concentrate on the fucking thing. There's a big apple biting contest going on in Apple Valley Village. In color. Thousands of kids and old folks are on their hands and knees biting apples.

Cora and I are in a sailboat. We've just left Casablanca, headed for Miami. The temperature and the wind are just right. We strip and I touch her soft tight skin. I lick every part of her body. She does the same to me. She's on her back, I enter her. Slowly, with visions of hoisting tackle, tubes, radar installations and conveyor belts, I move my hips in a circular motion. We change places. She's on top now. Moving back and forth. Quick short strokes. I close my eyes and see the white beach in Miami.

She can't sleep. She feels uptight. If you asked her to define anxiety she couldn't. She has bad dreams when she does sleep. She loses her personality when the dreams are really terrible. Her mind struggles through seaweed and garbage dumps. Her mental health, she worries about it. She wakes up mornings carefully counting her fingers and toes and her five senses. Tests her memory over and over. Talks quietly to herself. "I have an obsessional personality."

"No, Cora. You're cyclothymic."

"I'm schizo."

"You're Black and Marginal, emotional and fearful."

"No. I'm schizy."

"All right. Meditate then. And pray for sanity."

"Complexes complexes complexes."

"Go back to sleep."

"I haven't slept. Three days now and no sleep."

Sleep for me is never a problem. I have trouble understanding this aspect of Cora. I say, "Your mind is too busy."

"My soul. My horoscope says I can't be trusted."

"Fuck your horoscope. Have you ever been inside a mental hospital?"

"I've been inside a mental block."

"How about retardation."

"I used to think I was a genius or something." Cora covered her mouth with her right hand and laughed. "Just another casual factor of my derangement."

"You're depressed."

At this point I got up from the bed and sat on its side. "I wish sometimes I could develop amnesia."

"And forget Canada?"

"And Dale. And you too. And myself."

"Do you fear death?"

"I fear joy and love and anger and grief and, yes, I fear miracles. I . . . "

"Try to sleep." I stood up. Sighed.

I walked over to the window naked. Looked down at the people below walking on the street. The tops of cold painted cars. And felt a terrible fear gripping me.

In a play called *Voltage,* at an Off-Broadway theater called The New York Blackout of 1965, Cora is playing the part of a cottonwood tree. All she has to do is stand and slightly wave her arms. As her agent, I'm trying to book her for a part in a play to be staged in the auditorium in Megalopolis. After that I want to see her on the stage of the theater in Peking. In long running shows where scenes change fast. Shows with long chorus lines and lots of drum music.

In one sense Cora has to wait for me to tell her what to do, what to think. She hasn't changed and, yet, she changes all the time, right under my fingertip. Her sap flows. She's often like a tree, though she's never like a tree. No one is like a tree. I can't chew Cora's leaves. I take the words back. However I must trust I still know what I mean.

We spend too much time inside buildings, in rooms, in beds, with closed-in thoughts. Only once, I remember, we went to the country together, trees and grass, clear sky and insects. Unquestionably sincere moments. But I lose them when I try to bring them back, even for description. The image tries to represent something it is not. In it, I see Cora's large happy eyes. Glowing. If she speaks, she will speak as herself. I have only what I can handle: she has to handle her own joyful or painful words. Her tangible properties too. The day in the country, however, won't focus even enough for my newest techniques of inquiry; or, what some more critical self might term, "my deepening range of sensitivity." But I don't care, though I must or else.

I climbed a dingy short tree, filled with road dust, to see how far I could see; and Cora, lying on the unhealthy yellow grass. I can see her now—just a little bit of her, her eyes mostly. She has a blade of grass hanging from the right side of her mouth. From the fork in the tree, I saw nothing except the tops of other trees. No valley, no hills, no bluffs. Were we in New Jersey or upstate New York. Hardly matters. What does matter is the underglow I remember in Cora's smile. Away from closed-in rooms, closed-in thoughts. Away from the city and city noise and dirt and stink.

And I keep trying to bring the wholeness of this unquestionably human moment back. I like the warmth of such moments. But they get away and never come back, not even to say Hello. Twisted repressed moments fill their place. I sound like myself again.

I'm way back in my mind and I have no room to move around. It is crowded back here. Faces and hands and movements. I try to see how far I can see and I find only the inside surface of my brain. Cora is hiding behind the skin.

I'm a country preacher, a circuit rider. In the town of Hull I meet a gal named Cora. Knock her up and move on. A year later I hear about the child. Born dead. Fella named Canada marries Cora. Hear he's looking for me. Folks back in Tombstone say he's gunning for me. I go out West.

While taking a cable car ride over Squaw Valley I see Cora and Canada passing in the opposite direction. We wave.

The Concept West Village Theatre on Grove Street near Sheridan Square. Out front, on the white surface of the building, someone has hung a purple wreath. It clearly is to the memory of a "star" whose name decorated their playbills more than once. The circular form is spooky yet profound. In some way we'd usually rather not think about. Who is dead? Not a Broadway Angel. Not a Tombstone Rubber. Not a Sailboat Owner. And certainly not a Heart Researcher. But someone dear to the theater certainly. Some things we simply refuse to doubt.

The one whose caloric intake was never more than one thousand, eight hundred and seventy-five per day; whose birthplace was Atlanta, Georgia? Whose height was five-five, whose weight was one-twelve, at her best, one-twenty-five, at her distressing worst. Whose age, I would guess, was twenty-five. And whose occupation you already know. I'm beginning to feel like a fucking reporter. I owe you nothing. Actually I don't have to tell you anymore. I might even become an agent for Rolls Royce Owners. And start listening to "Like a Rolling Stone" every day. It all might get to be very spellbinding.

I try to stay loose. The Concept meant a lot to Cora Hull. Now it is pretty obvious she too meant just as much to it. "Eleanor Rigby," at this moment, from some car radio. A woman walks her blue twelve-year-old fox—no, it's supposed to be a dog. A sign in a window, "Parents of Gifted Children, Parents of Drug Users—UNITE—*talk to each other*!" It brings something like a smile to the edge of my mouth. Gas fumes are about to kill me.

I see Cora now in her black fur coat with side but-buttons and great deep pockets. But this time beneath it she wears an olive green dress.

The time we fucked backstage while Dale—or was it Canada?—was out front doing his part. She loves unusual events. She fears, most of all, boredom. *I think*. But what about me: I have a mildew odor and already I am no longer young. I remember how beautifully the audience responded each time. To her, to anybody. People in the audience: small company presidents, wine connoisseurs, sky divers, ex-addicts, anthropologists, tombstone rubbers, free-lance writers. Now, condolence. Circular motion. Surprise ending. Silly shit.

Cora is in a coffin. A group of thugs are transporting the wooden box to the East River. Four men in a black Cadillac.
Silently they drop it in, watching the ripples it leaves.
I must be one of them. I look at the other three. Their faces are not clear till we're back in the car and the ceiling light is on. One's not a man, but dressed in a man's dark hat and overcoat. It's Cora.

Cora is run over by a speeding taxi. She's lying in the street at the corner of Forty-second and Fifth. No blood in sight. The taxi stops halfway down the block, backs up and runs over her again. Hundreds of people are moving along the sidewalks, crossing at the corners. No one seems to notice. Suddenly I realize I am the driver. This becomes clear when I look in my rearview mirror, as I run over the body again.

Cora is in a play at The Concept. She's doing the finale. She's bringing the house down. She's turning the place out.

She goes on the road. She's in a bus with members of her company. One is playing a violin. Another sings an aria.

The bus stops. They go into a roadside restaurant for hamburgers. The waitress waits on Cora last. Before leaving she breaks a hundred plates, one at a time, against the mirror.

Outside, she finds a helicopter and flies back to New York.

I wear my tweed sport jacket a lot now. Not because *I* like it, Cora liked it. I walk by the theater every day now. I never did that before. I watch dog breeders on television. I try to avoid calling Canada. I even watch programs about ex-addicts. I think about Love and Hate and Anger and Joy. But a part of Canada is somewhere in the back of my mind. What will be the outcome of this investigation. It is no longer a spine-chiller. A classic tale of terror.

What would I like to do with myself now that Cora's absence makes decisions more difficult. Right this minute. I can almost touch her smile, her cheeks. Her wet lips excite me. Yet I feel I am shriveling . . . .

I close my eyes and she walks inside my skull. She turns fully into my trembling arms. She speaks. "I'm mean

and I'm poor. I'm a tramp, really a tramp. But I'm eminent!"
And her wet mouth sucks upward against mine. She makes a
quiet murmuring promise. I do not quite hear her nor do I
believe she is serious. My disbelief has something to do with
the secret look playing at the edges of her mouth. A certain
susceptibility. As though she knows fully the secret of nine
months of gestation in the womb. Cora, to say the least,
moves me too deeply.

"Don't promise me anything more."

"But, you remember, I scream when I'm mad."

"Is this extramarital love, Cora."

"No. It's instant Shock and Gothic and . . . "

"Hey! Stand back. You'll get hit by a passing car."

We pause at the curb only a few steps from the
theater. Cora is secretly grinning and clicking her tongue
against her teeth. I'm afraid to turn, to look back over my
shoulder, to see if the wreath of sorrow still hangs on the
white surface of the Concept West Village Theatre. Anyway,
there is a pause in the flow of traffic across the cobblestones,
and we instantly take advantage of it—with no idea of *where*
we are headed.

This novel has to keep changing. Hornbeam trees
should stand tall in it. Characters should beat drums. Beloved
friends should arrive at airports. Hackberry trees should be
used for firewood. Everyone should learn how to defuse a
bomb. The chorus line in every theater in New York should
be the beginning of a new novel. I want to take a stand. I am
like everybody.

The gross national product sleeps with the national
debt. A novel is anything. Fiction is a stained glass window.

We continue trying to do whatever it is we must do until we manage it. I tried to make up Cora many times before. Once as a flophouse molly singing, "Say It Loud—I'm Black and I'm Proud," dodging the police, sleeping with small company presidents, underground gourmets, ski-house hunters and science-fiction buffs, on a circuit from East Hartford and Bridgeport (during the jazz festivals), to Yonkers and Mount Vernon. Didn't work. Obviously. Another time I had her in Chicago, where I spent a lot of time. Depressing place and she didn't like it there either. I called her . . . *what was it?* Stella. Yeah, probably you never heard of her that way, under that name. Parts of her did however get into print, small circulation for only a few eyes. But this time she wasn't even dreaming of singing! "I Wish I Knew How It Would Feel to be Free"; and if *yourstruly* remembers correctly, much to his surprise, this was also the occasion on which she was casually and cynically involved with some very green young white man in the Black community working for his salvation and the crimes of the world. For free. But the way I have her now, I like her best. She's still herself and yet she's more mature, has more class, uses her head more to her own advantage, sees clearer; altogether, she's sharper, prettier, more elegant.

She works in many Off-Broadway plays, sometimes for as little as $10 per week; but it's what she wants to do, and Cora would be the last to complain. I see myself sitting on the window ledge watching her move with elegance about the room. I think we're in the theater, backstage. An unopened box of Ritz crackers is on the dressing table. A round carton of Wispride cheese, half eaten away, sits beside it. She doesn't eat properly and I can't convince her she should take vitamins and minerals. The pressure continues however. It spreads in many directions and it builds toward the center—its own . . .

Of course she flirted a lot. I had a time coming to terms with that aspect of her. It built a storm in the very center of my own frustration. I can't begin to tell you. Such pressure!

Selfish, self-centered people kill themselves; people who are focused on the light—or lack of light—at the end of the tunnel, kill themselves. Cora, Dale, Canada, the author, are based on nobody who would care to focus on anything. Scenes change. The chorus line changes. The girl in the box office changes. She goes home, searches the *Times* for another job. Balloons, in *New Yorker* stories, continue to float over the city. Cathedrals are sunk in smog. New York continues to be an interesting place.

"I didn't pay enough attention to her," said Canada. His right hand held a wine glass half filled with red dry wine. His elbow was against the red oak bar.

"You're bound to feel . . . "

The black leather of the stool, through my thin brown pants, was cool. A small hacksaw was lying on the bar. The bartender went to the jukebox and played, "Turn! Turn! Turn! (To Everything There Is a Season)."

Next to us at the bar were two middle-aged white men holding a conversation on mysticism and magic, superstition and meditation, faith and miracles. "Good grief!"

I could see Canada kissing Cora. No good. I tried to stop seeing it. I dreamed I saw one man using a hacksaw to cut off another man's arms.

A pair of tweezers and a pair of rubber gloves are lying on the bar. Someone across the room is laughing insanely.

"Did you know Cora?" Canada asked the bartender.

"There was this chick who used to shoot horse. She came in here like regular, you know. Wore real mink, bragged about it. Sometimes she had a black eye. Her old man never beat her though. Just had this habit of walking into things. Used to knock the shit out of herself. Carried a pair of pliers around in her purse. Think she was from Westchester or somewhere. It's really a shame, you know. I never see her anymore."

I watch Canada's wet eyes. He's drawing something invisible on the bar. And I suspect he's getting drunk.

"What was her name?"

The bartender went away toward a new customer.

Canada said it again. "Her name . . . "

Trying foolishly to cheer him I said, "Ultraviolet Light. She used to dance to 'Moon River.' Can't be Cora . . ."

"Let *him* tell me."

I watched the bartender take something to the new customer that looked like a glass of fountain pen ink, black. The customer was a woman, about forty, tired pale and over-dressed. When our eyes met she smiled, and though her smile was weak, it was not unfriendly, not frozen. I returned what I hoped was an equally generous smile, but by now she was already—so soon—gazing out the front window at the street.

Canada called the bartender. "Tell me her name!"

"Whose name?"

Cora is standing on line waiting to sign for an unemployment check. A man near the front starts crowing. A skinny woman in the middle begins to sing "The Star Spangled Banner." A fat woman at the end strips and stretches out on the brick floor with legs wide. A few men and women take turns on her. She's giggling and collecting payment for service rendered. In a pile alongside her are five and ten dollar bills, watches, rings and articles of clothing. The guard who looks like Canada, goes over to watch. He's dark red with embarrassment.

Cora has not returned and it is no longer warm; in fact, the warmth seems to have gone out of everything and all people. It must be freezing in here where I move around in my own space. Cora left a folded piece of paper (nothing on it) hidden under her bed. Canada found it and he still wonders. One day she was sitting naked on the bed, hot. I was browsing through her fancy titles. I couldn't find anything else to do, and that was the hottest day I can remember. No fan, no air-conditioner. At least I can't remember anything of the sort.

Cora stands on line in a bank waiting to cash her unemployment check. Two bank robbers enter with guns. Their faces are covered but Cora recognizes them anyway. They are obvious. Rather than collecting money from the tellers, they suddenly unload their Thompson Model 1921s, the twenty-round magazines falling, and run for a place on line. A little old lady, about eighty, takes out a .22-caliber, eight-shot revolver, and shoots them each four times. By now, Cora is laughing like crazy, while customers and tellers congratulate the old woman.

Canada's and Dale's bodies are carried out on stretchers by little men in streetsweeper suits.

The bank president jumps up on the counter and waves his arms. "Repeat after me everybody repeat after me: This bank will be forever safe from invasions from Canada or even Mexico. Let's hear it loud and clear!"

There was only stunned silence.

Cora was wearing dark pants. When she bent over to pick up the scraps, my eyes refused to pull themselves away from the underlying outline of her underpants.

"I never had a venereal disease," she said.

"It's going to rain." I got off my ass and helped her clean up the picnic area. "Look at the sky."

"Why did you ask me about sex?"

"I spoke of urinary infections because there was a burning sensation a moment ago while we were fucking."

"I'm not disabled."

"Cora," I said, painfully, "pick up the paper."

"I think you're right."

"Who left tobacco here?"

"Probably some smallpox victim. Cancer?"

"Pick up the shit, Cora."

"I *dare* you talk to me *in that tone of voice*!"

"Okay, okay."

We take the train back to the city. The Long Island Railroad is a dreary reality. Plus it is sort of cold. Too late in the year for a picnic. Cora and her mad ideas! I hope I don't wake up and discover something too terrible to talk about!

Cora and I are giggling and rolling together playfully in my place. She's trying to catch her breath and say something. I am aware of not wanting to hear her out. I lift her wet eyelids and spank her on the hip. With care everything here becomes obvious. Though it may take awhile. She tickles me under my arms and she screams when I touch her gently between her thighs. Her scream was not from trauma. She continues to murmur and bitch. She rolls and rolls. I scratch my way toward the center of the bed, naked. Sweating. Yet I know Cora means well as usual. "Let's come closer," she says.

Her hands are locked behind her arched back. Her earlobes are damp. She scratches one. I use the blunt pressure of my fist to open her soft lips, to examine her smooth teeth. Meanwhile she is making tracings on my stomach.

After awhile she is exhausted and, holding herself up on one elbow, she speaks. "Canada is endless."

"Never been there."

And she laughs too hard. Tears tears tears.

Cora and I are in bed somewhere. Fucking furiously. Canada comes in with a huge metal chastity belt. He knocks me over the head with it and, while I'm out, locks it securely around Cora's hips and between her legs. He drops the key into his pocket. I come to, in time to see him leaving.

I met this man who was afraid to sleep because he might dream something too terrible to speak of or even to remember. He said the dreams were always of a sexual nature, and in each was a woman who was very close to him; and not just physically. This woman was someone I too knew very well, he said. My mother? She wasn't my mother.

I couldn't remember my mother—but that's beside the point. First I had to discover who the man himself was. What he was dreaming and why.

We were both trying to hail a taxi on Broadway, downtown. We were both however headed uptown.

"Where do you live?"

He told me, "In you."

"Who are you?"

"I seek ways to improve my perception. I am ... "

"Double-talk. Then. Tell me, who is the woman."

"She's a Black woman from the South. Things fit into her. Her memory is good. She helps others. She has solutions and she can hit unseen marks. I'm trying to remember her."

"Can you remember her *name*?"

"*My* name is Jackson. But that name belongs to a lot of our people. All the way up to a point." In his voice was an undertone of annoyance. "She was called Hull. And incidentally she was also called Cora. I remember now ... "

"But now you're here, waving to passing cars."

"So are you."

"Well that's clear. I have to be *where* you are."

"So you be. So here I am."

"But where is this Cora ... ?"

"She has pain in the abdominal cavity. She's in some emergency room, crying."

"Then that's where you're headed ... "

"Precisely."

But no taxicab would stop.

A taxi stops for Canada. It takes him to the beach where Cora is naked, sitting in the sand. The sunlight is hot and the sky is clear. Cora's nipples are erect. Sand is stuck to her belly. Like jackels, a group of old men stand nearby watching her.

"You ready?"

They return to the city in the same taxi. Dale is driving. I own the taxi company. I'm in Florida on vacation.

Cora is in bed reading a bestseller and casually playing with her cunt. There are no good parts. I call her on the phone. "Repeat after me: There are no good parts."

"There are no good parts." She drops the bestseller.

"Are there good parts in Bangkok?"

"Are there good parts in Dick and Jane?"

I make too much of names; but then what are things or people *before* they attain names; Capricorn Cora Cove—I mean Hull; names. Tags signs symbols magic words. It isn't that my memory is all that bad. Though I am better at names than faces. Would probably be better the other way around. Cora was good involvement . . . . We were in a restaurant once. Sitting quietly resembling each other, not talking, not angry. But still under suspicion . . . . An obvious homosexual person entered and passed. Cora scribbled on a napkin: "She/he is cute." Which too was a way toward *naming*. Man *named* woman which condemned her to slavery. I see blue colors blending into each other, sadness. I try to learn to forgive people. Even the cops who scraped up her blood deserve sympathy. Or the world is a pile of shit. Even monsters who copulate with their victims, forgive forgive! Everything everybody continues to move in a humorous circle around and back . . . .

Otherwise I'd have to stop at a particular point. I would perhaps even spend more time trying to cultivate a true friendship with Canada. Who continues to brood, without any sincere loss of love. But I can't decide whether or not he needs to be alone. He scratches his legs a lot and he sniffs. Tries not to think about his *own* presence. He gives up easily. But then there's so little to cling to. I handle him all right at times. Largely though, he handles himself better. Tragic, because he doesn't truly know even basic things about himself.

I'm tired of Canada; I'm tired of his grief and his self-pity; but I have trouble trying to make him leave my head alone. Inside my head things refuse to stop touching each other. People move around in it and Canada stands out. Hidden behind his dark glasses. Cora got sick and tired of him too. And after all she loved him. And never pretended otherwise, even in my arms.

Cora and I are in bed drinking gallons of dry white wine, eating cheddar cheese grapes nuts and oranges.

The phone rings. She answers. I can hear the voice on the other end. "There's a traffic jam outside. Best to take the George Washington Bridge."

Cora says, "You have the wrong number." Her mouth is full of grapes.

The voice again, "Do not enter. Repeat: Do not enter."

"Hang up, baby, let's eat!" I drink from the bottle. I take a huge bite of cheddar. It smells stinky good. I wash it down with wine.

"At the pedestrian crossing there's an accident," says the voice. "Drive with care. No passing. Nobody has right of way. This is *not* a recorded message. This is your life. Repeat after me: This is a place where you must proceed with caution."

Suddenly, I took the phone from Cora and hung it.

Each situation does something desperate to my nerves—causes me to drive and struggle on to the next one. I stumble over the shattered pieces of the suitcase. I keep dreaming I sprinkle white powder in an oblong area.

Is it the illusion of peace I seek. Had a round with *that* myth! Know now that the real point is to deal with the situations and scenes. And I must stop watching television in an attempt to avoid the pain of memory. Dull shit.

I can see a little better than before. Yet I still have only *this* particular kind of vision.

Does the suitcase found at the scene of the "crime" mean that Cora was planning to run off with Dale? The thought is too depressing. I take a trip to get away from it. Somewhere between Dry Hill and Watertown, New York I check into a motel to watch TV. I see Cora in a Black Theatrical Company production. She's playing the part of a Black Greenwich Village actress named Cora Hull . . .

I'm on the road again, with the interstate system running through my blood. The ghost of Dale sleeps in the trunk of this rented Toyota. I hit the Adirondack area. In Old Forge, I stop and play a game of tennis with a foxy suntanned white woman, mother of two small boys. Cora suddenly turns up in the court alongside us, playing with Dale. On horseback, Canada comes onto the beach, standing at the fence, watching the game. When they aren't looking, I sneak away. Continue north. The Toyota runs out of gas at Blue Mountain Lake. I fall in love with a hippie chick and we have twins, girls. She clings too tightly. I leave her and continue . . .

I try not to see in segments. Cora is whole. Canada is whole. Dale attempts to be whole. He is whole regardless of my inability to see him whole. Like the others he is living tissue. And they all play games. Canada, for example, played a terrible trick on Cora. I can't remember what it was but I remember her anger. She always had a hard time with crucial moments in games. Not just card games. Real life games. Dale, though I suspect he is *a game* to her, is another matter.

Sometimes I try to see nothing, but even nothing has its *content*. Each of them has too much trouble at times. I get fucking sick. Cora's desperation. Canada's questions. Dale's elusiveness. I'd rather come to terms with the rubber plant in the kitchen. Talk to it. Wait for it to answer. But I hear loud French horns again and again and children, running across snow outside, screaming and laughing.

I remember laughing at Cora in a play on a stage. When was that. Plastic pink furniture. She was playing a frustrated bitchy wife married to a newly successful business-man, Negro. She was fearful he'd fall any moment. She couldn't deal with the lack of security in his success—and though no one else thought it funny, I couldn't stop laughing. I laughed so endlessly that I blindly engineered my way out of the theater and stood in the lobby giggling and feeling terrible and self-conscious. A young man who introduced himself as an electronics engineering student came over and asked if there was anything he could do. And all I could do was laugh louder. Cora and Canada and Dale are still in the other room seated around the card table waiting for me. And I can't go back.

The four of us are playing cards again to the sounds of Scott Joplin's piano. Roman soldiers break in. They say

Agatha Christie sent them. They drag Cora outside and nail her to a cross planted in the sidewalk. Dale, Canada and I are helpless as we watch. When they finish, the leader takes a sea shell from his pocket, speaks into it, "All finished boss! What's the next assignment?" The sea shell says, "Make her scream! Light matches to her toes!" At this point, I erase the soldiers and the cross. Cora comes down gently, unharmed. I kiss her and say, "Don't ever trust Santa. And for God's sake, stay away from Roman soldiers!"

Cora is in a small town in Georgia, somewhere outside Atlanta. She's tied up in the back seat of a police car. Fifty white cops are gang raping her as she struggles to free her arms and legs. She can't make it. While the last cop is opening his pants, a boy child slides out of Cora's vagina, grows up instantly. A big, strong young man. Suddenly, he starts beating the shit out of the fifty cops. With his bare fists he beats them into a pile of pulp. He releases his mother then vanishes.

A white cop knocks a picket sign out of Cora's hand. Grinds it beneath his big black boot. "WE DEMAND EQUAL RIGHTS NOW" no longer clear. Anger swells her temples. She scratches her left cheek furiously, mulch beneath her nails. She is a young girl in jeans and she fights back her mosaic of tears. She is in the middle of an aggregate of changes. Her eyes hurt. She is beginning to understand something called the Competitive Exclusion Principle and not just in terms of ecological science. Now she really understood why she'd come South to Atlanta, her birthplace, to march, demonstrate, like this. No more dancing in night halls—her life's work from this point on was decided: she would be a revolutionary! No more lipstick nylon douche nozzles or fingernail polish. She had to become a non-combustible person. Build an inner framework that could easily absorb not only pain but also endless shock . . . .

But she *did* dance in night halls again, and she worked behind New York City office typewriters before she made it on the Off-Broadway stage. "You a mammyfucker, baby!" Canada told her time and again. "A mammyfugger . . . sugar!"

She nearly stripped one night in a dance hall the music got so good to her. But Canada slapped her, bringing her back to her senses. And she sat sulking.

And as Canada dragged her home through the moulded night she looked, to herself in a plateglass window, like a flat piece of plastic fabric. Synthetic resin. She knew she was drunk and she kept her mouth shut, not wanting to risk contact with the impact of Canada's fist.

Then that fatal day. She is standing on the other side of the street, cautiously. Trying not to look obvious. She begins to walk slowly. Secretly spying on the windows of nearby houses. Guilty. She also looks up desperately at the sky. And as she reaches the house in which no one lives, she is already wet . . . She enters, unaware that her death is only a few moments away.

I'm the undertaker. To get away from being the undertaker, I change places with the tour guide. I take people through many changes, across state lines, into new time zones; we stop at traditional points of interest, on scenic roads, and in state waysides. When I'm sick of guiding, I return to Cora. And Canada. And myself. And these words. This book.

Cora is in a large bright room with a lot of naked people. She's naked too. They're all screwing and kissing and doing other interesting things to each other.

Cora says to the man on top of her "I thought this was supposed to be a sensory awareness center?"

He grunts. "We're all going to die soon. Repeat after me: We're all going to die soon. Hold me close."

She doesn't mind the wild things screaming from the inside of her brain as long as she has her wonderful rafters to walk beneath. Even the grand furniture, redwood or rosewood or otherwise, Cora can live without. She could go about her business in her house with its Gallic accent in Westchester County or in New London and not give another thought to the outside world. So she thinks. So she dreams. The rafters above her and the fireplace in the big living room, and the other stuff can wait. She'd even move in without a bed. She dreams openly of this when she stands outside the door looking at the dreary New York street where she lives. Where she is beside herself. Cora is waiting for something; yes, she waits for the thing that is some entity or nonentity always slightly ahead of her, eluding her, leading her. But she continues to wait because there is nothing else she can do. And having no alternatives, she escapes in her elegant cardigan evening gown, through the forest to her country house with its good prints in frames on the walls, a house with a worn-out wheel of a farm manure spreader for a chandelier above her dizzy, happy head . . . . Though this too is a form of waiting.

She can't take Canada with her because the house she dreams isn't on his list. He believes only in the things on his private list. She'd thought of taking Dale along, but in the long run he wouldn't like it either. A city type.

I don't think she even considered me or she gave up on me the moment she rejected the idea of possibly taking Canada along.

Now Canada is alone.

Take my word for it: he is very much alone *and* frightened. You don't have to think about it to realize it. One remembers one's own aloneness. Yet he continues to make lists, though not of demolition weapons. Grocery lists now; and lists of things to do. Usually before going to bed to sleep each night he'll make a list of things to do the following day. Or he will do it the first thing in the morning. Mainly, the energy put into this goes toward establishing some *reason, any* reason—doesn't matter how small—for *continuing*. And the lists so far get him through. One uses whatever one has. If it takes a list each day, it takes a list. For someone else a list might be the worst thing possible.

He blows his nose, he brushes his teeth; and very shortly, he sells his shotgun. Yet Canada is not known for selling his personal effects. He used to pawn his goods when he was desperately poor. Before the day he turned actor.

Always it was clear he possessed more than he or anyone else could ever touch or smell or hear. The weapons were the least of it. After Cora, they meant so little. Love seems to always take the forefront. It needs space. It needs time and it needs *a certain wildness, a kind of carelessness*!

Even after she died—was found dead—Canada tried and tried to pretend she was alive: "Cora went to the laundry to drop off some sheets."

"I'm depressed," he said to himself. Went over to the window and looked down upon the street. I envy nobody.

Canada has to get away. He rents a Mack truck and, dressed like a truck driver, he hooks it to a trailer filled with traditional and realistic American novels by Black and white authors. He drives north. In Buffalo he stops to eat a hot dog and an order of french fries at a roadside restaurant. While he's eating, another customer, a man with a French accent, whispers in his ear, "You're on the right track." At Plattsburgh, Canada picks up a hitchhiker. A blond girl wearing a raincoat, nothing on under it. She has lovely blue eyes. She goes down on Canada while he's driving. In the next town they marry and settle down. It takes ten years for their neighbors to accept them. At this point, they move on north to Quebec where Canada learns French and politics. His wife goes to college and learns how to teach college. He calls her Cora.

"Would you people kindly step outside," the beef-red police captain said. "Please people!" As he spoke his thick pink fingers pushed at their backs. They moved.
"Draw a line around the bodies."
"Why?"
"Because in the movies they do it."
Somebody laughs. "Nothing's funny."
"You too, young man, please—*outside!*"
But I said to him: "I want her . . . I mean, I want to draw a line around *her* body, myself. I don't trust you people."

They laughed at me.

"Outside, sonny."

"You seem to forget *I control you,* motherfucker!"

"So you control me. Please go."

"Suppose I refuse . . . ."

"You won't."

"What makes you so sure?"

"*Listen,* you're wasting my time!"

Another cop spoke up: "He knows you'll leave because if you don't *you* yourself can't *go on.*" He laughed and took out a fresh cigar, bit off the tip, wet it halfway along its length, lit it.

Outside the door the boy in the green shirt stood with his mouth hanging open.

"Nice and cozy in there, huh?"

Cora takes the boy in the green shirt with her to a women's consciousness raising group. At the door they stop her.

"What's the story?"

Cora tells the young white woman, "He's in great need of your message."

"You can come in but he can't."

Cora and the boy leave.

At another women's liberation meeting they are admitted. On the floor, two women are fucking.

A lesbian is standing on a table, giving a lecture. "Listen, sisters, we're being accused of being dykes and wanting to be like men. Gotta fight this shit! How'd the Puerto Rican kid get in?" She's pointing a finger at the boy. "Throw him out!"

Cora leaves with the kid.

Cora and the boy wander around for hours trying to think of something to do. They finally go to see the movie, *Deep Throat*. The audience is in stitches. The boy starts crying.

Cora takes the child home. She leaves him in the hallway. She climbs the steps.

As she goes up, she can hear the kid's mother opening the door and asking, "Where you been?" and the boy saying, "Around the world, around the world!" And the mother says, "Get ya ass in here before I stomp you!"

I'd be willing to build my dream house of adobe but Cora insists on modern materials. Canada says, "Give me azulejos." And Dale says, "I'll take ashlar." But what would you decorate it with, Cora? She says, "Acanthus." Then she thinks about it a bit more. Speaks again: "No. Ornamentation, I don't want." Canada says, "How about in your tomb, your grave, your casket." She laughs. "Just me." Dale laughs too. "My death should be ornamented with antifixae-style materials." "How about Aztec?" "No," he said. "Cora, does meat have style?" She never answered: turned into a rabbit and jumped away into a bush. Green wetness.

I wake and I realize I have enough good things going to counterbalance the bad. I suppose one important thing I should always realize is that *things are not always things*. Especially not the things I'm talking about. I may not be actually speaking.

I study The International Phonetic Alphabet, but I can't sincerely say I learn it. I study Cora, but not with the insult of anthropological thought. Nor the folly of some aspects of Freudian wisdom. I still don't know who Cora is or what Canada or Dale meant to her. In her black coat she is another person.

Still, I take care when I wake up in the morning. Cora isn't here. But it doesn't matter: believe *that* if you like; I get up slowly with great care. I must protect my head. Save it. Keep it from the danger of the devils, the monkies . . .

Cora is away. She's twelve in Atlanta with her father. They're walking along Butler Street. A white man bumps into Cora's father. "Don't you know how to step aside for a white man, nigger?" Cora's father smiles. The smile jumps off Mr. Hull's face and stabs Cora through the chest. The pain stays with her. Meanwhile, Mr. Hull steps aside for the white man.

Cora, her mother and father are sitting at the dining room table eating supper. Cora syas, "A white man attacked daddy today." Mrs. Hull gave her husband a quick fearful glance then told Cora, "Lies are bad for the soul, child. You tell lies you get lost in them. Repeat after me: My father is a brave and strong man and nobody pushes him around."

"My father . . . "

Truly it is a good very fine thing that she stuck with Drama—with a capital D—to the end. Not its end. I feel sure it serves a purpose. Knowing it helps us move into her. Have you noticed we are moving in closer now. The space she left us in which to move begins to narrow, but that's all right. Anyway by now I think you find no problem realizing this is her eulogy. Someone had to do it. It is the death of the old life. But we still hear her murmuring. Onstage her words are soft and you can nearly read her thoughts. She tries so hard. Certainly she should make the grade. I keep thinking she is still up there moving about.

It is obviously a liberating job, with its inlets; it is definitely an outlet for Cora. The script though is not at all easy. Yet she is a natural. She makes her transitions smoothly. I should take lessons from her.

Canada probably wouldn't have gone into the theater if it had not been for Cora's influence. Her excitement. She generated so much energy when it came to the theater of her experience. Though Canada is not the absolute image of the Supreme Father, he will do for a stage appearance. He knows how to put in a good one, and it saved him from poverty and dreary jobs and muck and pure shit and mops in hallway closets all night in apartment buildings. It saved him from flushing cigarette butts down toilet stools in bus stations, from slapping a cotton rag across some old man's expensive leather shoes. He might have turned into rubber or a sponge. But he met Cora and took up acting. In Negro slang an actor is a bullshit person, a fake.

Dale broke records on the stage too. But Canada I respect, in his crudeness, in his glory, in his small mean talent. I try not to assess the range of his vision. I'd rather give him a brotherly slap on the shoulder. To touch him without fear of losing my manhood. I know I feature large in his dreams. Another thing I know: for him Cora is the Supreme Woman. There are some qualities in her as woman he would not want to see her overthrow. But as I say, Dale too broke records and he broke plates and bottles—even on Cora's clean floor. His acting was not confined to the legitimate stage. But then nothing legit was confined to him. Good ol' Dale!

Before the stage however he earned a living by licking floors in supermarkets and the long hallways in office buildings in midtown in the wee hours of the night. That was when he was young and could take it. He was lucky he made it. The guys he worked with in those days still do it today and they're no longer young.

But Cora's orientation, you know, was different. She came from somewhere else. And she was always smoothly coming to this place, the stage. Where she now stands, the broken pieces of glass all around her feet. I can't make it any plainer. It would mean stopping too many more times. And then you would have to go out and bring me examples. Anything you could find.

They all finally worked well in groups. You will see what I mean.

Cora is fifteen in Atlanta. Her father is telling her the history of Black people. Pride in his voice. When he finishes, Cora says, "Am I more than Black?"

"Tomorrow I will teach you how to do calculus."

And he did. He taught it well. And she learned well.

She looks like her father. His thoughts keep leaping into her mind. They enter her body through her eyes, not her ears.

Cora is visiting her grandparents in a small town outside Atlanta. Her grandmother says, "Keep your dress down." Her grandfather says, "You're cute little thing."

Back at home, Cora sees her mother scrubbing and cooking and washing dishes and singing spirituals. "Mama, are you sad?" Her mother smiles.

Cora's father is driving her to the hospital to have her tonsils removed. "Remember, Cora, what I tell you is right."

Cora is sipping the thick liquid from the bottle. Between sips she holds it up to the light, shakes it, watches it foam.

I am putting on my pants, looking around for my shoes. It's late or it's early. I am possessed by restlessness. Cora sighs then breaks into a fit of coughing; her face turning purple. Can I help her. She's sitting there in her slip in the armchair. She seems to be gaining weight. Right before my eyes.

"I want to look at just *one side* of your face."

"But why, Cora."

"While I take the hairpins from my hair."

"I'll sit on the rug and watch."

"Turn a little, will you. Yes, like that."

"How is this."

"Yes, but more."

"More?"

"No. Just think gently now."

"About what?"

"About electronic scanners and test-tube babies and . . . your growth. Your balance."

"You're making fun of me again."

"But I take my fun seriously."

"Cora, you're too serious."

Cora is a very serious secretary in a Madison Avenue office. The Secretary of State enters. He states his business. He's looking for the Ford Foundation. Cora tells him he's in the wrong building. He says he's looking for America. She tells him he's getting warm. He takes off his necktie. The Secretary of State is getting mad. "Let me see the boss!" Cora rings the boss. He comes out, shakes hands with the Secretary of State. Cora pretends to type something serious while listening to their conversation.

Boss: You vote for me, I make you rich.

Secretary of State: I vote for you. Can you give me some women too.

The boss: I give you women like you never seen.

The Secretary of State: How about the one at the typewriter over there?

The boss: Sure, sure no problem. You like a few boys for dessert? I got boys and half-boys too. You name it, I got it!

After work Cora goes home. The Secretary of State is standing in front of her apartment door, grinning. "Hi."

"Hello." She feels a draft. "What's your problem?"

"I simply want to apologize for the crude conversation you obviously overheard today." He chuckles. "Also, to explain to you that I am *not* the Secretary of State. I am Jack the Ripper and I plan to rip you."

At this point, he falls to his knees and starts crying.

Do you know there are plants that move about in deep silence and warm rocks that live with emotions of their own; babies born to the male of the species and . . . Cora is interested in the sea and babies. I have some interest also. But I'm more interested in gadgets and hooks than I used to be.

I'm more patient with mystery novels too. It has to do with coming closer to the point, and also with what some people call maturity. I don't call it anything. I now send my "name" out for Trial Examinations. It doesn't matter what the product is. That's beside the point. The point now is I can do it without frustration. Even at times with a certain excitement. I ordered "deep silence" for Cora; and I ordered several tiny emotional rocks too. If I don't like the products I can send them back for a complete refund. I suspect however I'd have to pay them for shipping and handling. I can't imagine them not getting something out of me. And another thing I do more than ever now is rest. I rest well and long and deeply. In deep silence. The gadgets and hooks all around my bed. Under the bed I keep a pan of water. With it I breathe easier. The air is dry, you know.

At times I still want to go away but it isn't Cora's fault anymore. She isn't here. She can't make me. No more broken pieces of her spirit to try to glue together again. I still watch television though. It's black and white. My eyes take better to black and white. To sit before the set, lost in it, is like moving on to another place—if only for a short while.

Changes. Nothing seems to stop changing; things slide or bump into other things. I can't speak anymore. For a long time I had trouble even lifting my voice to a normal pitch. Then I went out and talked for a long time to a lot of people. I got sick of speech and now I whisper slowly, gently. And there is no one to hear. No eye to behold my changes, the mystery of my moods.

It's Thanksgiving Day. Cora has cooked a large turkey. It's on the kitchen table. She has no dining room. She is alone with the stuffed bird. She sits there looking at it. Cora feels sad, empty. If only she had a dozen children. What about the kid in the green shirt? Heck, his mother probably cooked a turkey also.

Cora begins to nod. The turkey begins to move. Its movements wake her. She's alarmed and runs from the apartment screaming for help.

Alarmed by her screams, the neighbors also enter the hallway. Cora is jumping up and down, beating her fists against her face. *"The turkey is talking! The turkey is talking! The turkey is talking!"*

They take her to Bellevue. She's under observation for fifteen days. They release her. Say she's normal. Normal?

Did I tell you the boy in the green shirt was run over by a speeding car. In a side street. One block from where he lived. Cora told me, tears in her eyes. Someone knocked at her door to tell her. She remembers putting a finger to her lips. The sunlight was lean that day. When she came back into the room and told me the news my mind was tight with knots. At first it didn't register who she was referring to. The name slushed back and forth.

Then. I remembered Canada's reaction to the kid. Was it jealousy. I can understand jealousy. Someone knocks at the door with jealousy. People finger each other with jealousy. Cora shakes her pretty head with jealousy. The boy in the green shirt lay dead on the street, out of a style of jealousy. But I won't miss him because I didn't know him.

"I have to get my mind off things," Cora said. "I'm going to the kitchen and count the silverware again."

"Polish it."

"You polish yourself. I have to stop thinking. He was a lovely boy."

"Where is your teddybear?"

"I have a headache. Please don't ask. Let me be to myself."

She is walking in a circle stopping only once by the window to look out. This obviously is more than a crucial moment. I feel the distance between Cora and myself. Where is Canada. She turns from the window as I am about to leave. Her eyes are nervous twitching points.

Going out, I touch the blue and pink flowers. Soon they too will be dead. The doorway smells of rotten wood and rainwater. The street, of gasoline. Gas fumes and smoke. As I walk toward the subway entrance I am conscious of the space around my body. Too conscious. I remember Cora's feeling that eyes everywhere were watching her. Her guilt.

You see, I can handle myself better now that the end is close. I have spent more time in Canada too. Dale still has not received justice. You can't be all things to all people. There's too much conflict. Even when I handle myself well the conflict grows—it narrows in one way and expands in another.

A man is on top of Cora about to stick his cock into her cunt. She's terrified. The thought is painful. She's not ready. She gently pushes him away. "Go away, man." With his erection, he finds it difficult to go away peacefully. He argues, whines, begs. Cora says, "Go!"

Like a whipped dog, he goes.

Another man is behind Cora. She's on elbows and knees, naked. Somewhere on some bed. She's not ready. The man tries to enter her. "No, no, not yet." But he's very excited and he doesn't listen to her. He tries desperately to enter. When it goes in, it causes a shortage, the lights go out, and there's an electrical burn at the tip. The man runs from the motel room screaming.

On the subway train men are grabbing Cora's ass, squeezing it, pinching it. She fights them off with her purse.

They follow her home and invade her sleep. With erect cocks, they trot wildly across her breasts.

Cora goes to the hospital to have her breasts cut off. They are cancerous. The next day the breasts grow back. More erect, lovely, with firm bright nipples.

Men start following her everywhere she goes. She takes a German P-38 Automatic in her purse. When she tries to shoot it nothing happens.

The cops are coming to an end too. I meant to tell you that before now. They might easily have come to their end a little while ago. When they come they have their equipment with them. This is a slow painful notice of their worth, though not an assessment.

The cops, you will notice, are easy to handle, particularly since they have no personalities to speak of. I wouldn't speak of them even if they had something worth speaking of. I don't have space. And my purposes are not treacherous. They are simply minor characters, not symbols of Apollo at Rhodes: which is the way I suspect they would describe themselves.

Like his father, I think Canada was a cop for a brief time. You can feel the coolness of Canada. Colossus, black in blue, behind the impressive metal of a badge! Get to it! Yet he's so far from it. Can even enjoy Thanksgiving Day Independence Day even New Year's Day!

Cora is married to a policeman. They have a house in Queens. He has ten thousand dollars in the bank. Cora does the laundry. Cora cooks dinner. The policeman wears his gun at all times. He tells her, "Be careful." They have two children Bobby and Jim.

One night the policeman comes in and shoots up the joint. When he runs out of bullets, Cora asks, "What's the matter?"

"I want some excitement around here."

His children crawl into bed and fall into a deep sleep.

Cora goes out. She walks the streets looking for a trick.

Her cop husband at home watches television till he fades into the screen.

There's no doubt about it: everything Cora does happens first in my mind. Here she is out in Wyoming. She's wearing boots studded with diamonds and she's strutting around, a badass cowgirl, determined to teach cowpokes a real lesson . . . in compassion.

On the main street in Cheyenne, Wyoming you can buy guns and leather skirts, boots and saddles.

I run the funeral parlor. I dig the graves. I help deliver babies. The shit will never stop hitting the fan. I run the police station. I'm the doctor in emergency. I make the last judgment.

Cora lives in an old New York brownstone. An army tank has stopped in front of it. Soldiers are standing around the tank, holding M-1s. I'm throwing them in to keep the tank company. Canada and Cora are coming down the steps to the sidewalk. You can look at their faces and see they're not surprised to see the tank or the soldiers. You'd think they were in a city in Vietnam in the middle of the war. "Morning, fellas!"

Cora speaks: "I'd rather watch the *Newlywed Game* or *As the World Turns.* I don't want to die. I'd rather shop in cheap dimestores, decorate my home with crepe paper, blues, yellows, reds; I'd much rather go shopping for elegant buys, bonuses, hidden angles. Or teach myself needlework. I'd even settle for something so simple as *Magilla Gorilla.* I'd give myself to a member of the British Commonwealth of Nations, make love 19,785,000 times in 3,690,410 beds and kiss him goodbye in Ottawa, and think no more of it."

"You simply refuse to go into details," I said.

She looked sharply into my blinking eyes. "You're too much like Canada. You don't understand me. Who am I really. Oh, sure. You *know* my home address; my telephone number; my marital status; you probably know something about my health; the name of the high school I attended, the year of my academic diploma, my high school activities, that I sang in the campy chorus and served as one of the editors on the school's literary magazine." She paused.

And somewhere in my senses, I searched for some clue to what she really meant.

"And what did I do in college. You know. I hate to even think about it. But you still don't know me."

"You're silly."

"I want to be *known* before I die! What's silly about that? I want immortality! And what I did in college won't give it to me. Who cares about my twenty-six credits, my major, my minor, my scholarship from the state's regents, my average, my activities, the workshops I took; who cares that I tutored poor, undereducated Black kids in the Black community and that I *had* a very white attitude toward what I was doing. Who cares? Huh ... I even took a few courses in teacher training—actually thought of becoming a teacher! Me! Can you believe it?"

"This, I believe."

We are lying in my bed, her head on my shoulder. The room is dark blue and stuffy. My facial skin feels tight.

"I even took a modeling course at a charm school. Gave that up. And after that all kinds of shit jobs, I think you know. One shit job after another. Now. Where in all of this is the clue to immortality?"

"Sorry," I say, "you simply have to die first, then be reborn, then go to heaven, and there, know peace forever."

"Stop playing with me, will you. I'm serious."

Saying nothing, I hoped to indicate to her I wanted her to go on. But she lay there breathing heavily against me. I loved her. I love her still.

"Then, I wanted to improve my chaces in this man's world, so there was that terrible silly time with that wild screwedup correspondence course: memory improvement, learn-while-you-sleep, speedwriting. You know the scene!"

I laugh a little bit for her.

She continues: "After that shit fell through I had a new brainstorm: I'd become a fashion designer. (Now, see all the while in the back of my mind I knew I was an actress, knew I belonged on the stage or better still, on the screen! But I didn't have the guts to make that plunge! Nevertheless, I wore out a copy of *My Life in Art* by Stanislavski. Oh, I devoured *books* on acting and the theater! *Theatre Ethics of Stanislavski, The Method of K. S. Stanislavski and the Physiology of Emotions,* I wore out those two too! And every magazine of the theater I could get my hands on. But, somehow, I'd been brainwashed into thinking my thoughts of the theater as a career were not practical, so . . .) I enrolled in a dress design school. After one month I gave it up. Anyway before I finally made the plunge—I was still in Atlanta—I messed around with a few other correspondence schools wasting time. Then one morning I woke up and said to myself, 'Cora, you're going to New York, honeychile'—and I did, that very day!"

"How was New York in the beginning?"

"I couldn't begin. I kept suddenly appearing in the mirror, tears in my eyes. I felt crazed."

"Did you comfort yourself with Stanislavski?"

"No, I started drinking vodka. With a little of my own perspiration. I was learning my lines all right."

"How did you find your way?"

"In fragments. It's too painful to talk about. Your questions make me sound like somebody like Dorothy Dandridge who's just retired from an exotic career of saloon singing."

"Hold your head up a minute, baby, I got to get up, go pee."

My words were unexpected, and she was stunned, and actually couldn't move for a moment.

When Cora moved she moved mountains.

She always wanted more than one man to make love to her at once. She told herself this.

Cora is being fucked by three men at the same time. What does she feel?

Cora is alone in a house with one man. What does she feel?

I'm the undertaker, the gravedigger, the gentle doctor in emergency, the judge in the garden of earthly delights! I talk holy shit and giggle in the middle of serious problems. This book is pulling itself together. It turns and turns. Here it is again.

The dirty windows break, flying away. And there is this ring of echoes. Bone blood eardrums the slime of eyes. The skin slides quietly from the muscle. But the embrace continues. Cora continues. Dale was never meant to make it.

He was that side of myself that should be rewritten. Dale was an argument I had with the past.

Here I am touching the words that touch his face and hands. They do not fit into the blank space that is Dale. When I stop making this thing the thing remains. I never did mean for Dale to cling to the idea of himself. There is no thought here for him to hold. The pieces break into smaller pieces. Cora cannot hold on to me. She cannot see Dale. At this point she is unaware of herself. The pressure holding them together is so great it cannot be measured.

I suck her tongue and lick her hairline. I bite her neck and run my tongue into her cunt. Up the crack of her ass. This way I know she is still living. She strokes my hair and whispers, "Oh, Canada, oh baby."

Canada has melted into an abstraction. Even so he is still concrete. Dale was never anything but a word. I'm fed up. I want to get rid of them.

Cora wanted to get out of herself. She is sleeping. I kiss her ear. Lick the hair under her arm. She is running away across a desert. The sand is hot. The sky is black. She is almost out of herself. She falls on hands and knees. Dale arrives on a camel with a message from Canada. He reads it through a loudspeaker: "As you run, remember, a shadow settles over my spirit. You understand that, Cora, and you understand how I will move through it to the clearing I seek. If only I could wrap wet towels around the broken pieces of the shadow. But that might not do it. If I could deal with the beginning and the ending a little better. Still that might not do it. Even to invent another name for myself won't do it. It's strange, the clearer things get the less it matters. Even the shadow doesn't matter."

Dale gives Cora a hand. At the edge of the desert they step into the city. They step into a house. It explodes. It is a device. I am responsible. I set the device.

Canada calls me. With the phone an inch from my ear I listen: "Once you stop there isn't likely to be any thing left. Otherwise it would not be time to stop."

With my bare hands I break the phone. Canada is still talking to me through the pieces. I throw them on the floor and kick them.

About the Author

Clarence Major is the prize winning author of eleven books. His fiction and poetry have been translated into Italian, French, German and other languages. Major's short works have appeared in a variety of anthologies and magazines. He teaches creative writing and literature, most recently at Brooklyn College, CUNY.

FICTION COLLECTIVE

Books in Print

The Second Story Man by Mimi Albert
Searching for Survivors by Russell Banks
Reruns by Jonathan Baumbach
Things in Place by Jerry Bumpus
Museum by B.H. Friedman
Reflex and Bone Structure by Clarence Major
The Comatose Kids by Seymour Simckes
Twiddledum Twaddledum by Peter Spielberg
98.6 by Ronald Sukenick
Statements: New Fiction, edited by Fiction Collective authors